WHAT ABOUT WILL

WHAT ABOUT WILL

ELLEN HOPKINS

G. P. Putnam's Sons

G. P. Putnam's Sons

An imprint of Penguin Random House LLC, New York

Copyright © 2021 by Ellen Hopkins
Excerpt from *Closer to Nowhere* © 2020 by Ellen Hopkins

G. P. Putnam's Sons is a registered trademark of Penguin Random House LLC.

Visit us online at penguinrandomhouse.com

Library of Congress Cataloging-in-Publication Data is available.

Manufactured in Canada
ISBN 9780593108642

1 3 5 7 9 10 8 6 4 2
FRI

Design by Eileen Savage
Text set in Amrys

For everyone who has lost someone they love.
I hope you were able to find them again.
If you haven't, keep looking.

My Big Brother

Always
had a
short
fuse
but now
                    it's permanently lit.

Okay, it was never
hard to set Will off.

It used to be a game
I played, mostly
just for kicks.
It was funny, watching
the blood throb
in his temples.

But sometimes,
when trouble
was staring at me
and I wanted to aim
it in a different direction,
I'd rile Will up
until he blew.

Then, when Mom
or Dad started griping
about my behavior,
I'd point at my brother,
all red-faced and cussing,
and ask, "What about Will?"

I never thought
I'd get sick
of that question.

Check It Out

It's been a long time
since I've said it straight
to my brother's face,
but I love him, wicked
bad temper and all.

We used to be best-
friend brothers.

Will's seventeen, which
makes him five years
older, and I've always
looked up to him.

Mostly because
he never looked
down on me.

When I was like
four, and most other
kids still rode tricycles,
Will took the training wheels
off my little blue bike
and taught me to ride it.

> *You can't keep up on four
> wheels, Trace,* he said.

Even on two, it took a while,
but eventually, I did.
At least, I came close.

Will also helped me
learn how to
      Rollerblade
         skateboard
           and, best of all, snowboard.

My first time on the slopes,
I guess I was six.
Mom took Will and me.
      Dad stayed home.

I remember he said
he had to work, but later
I found out he's not
real big on cold weather.

      Why do you think we live
      in the desert? he asked.
      If I wanted to be miserable,
      I'd move back to Minnesota.

Sometimes I can't believe
I'm related to him, even though
I've got his curly brown hair
and gold-speckled eyes.

But I loved snow the minute
I saw it, all crisp and sparkly,
like quartz crystals in the sun.
As for the cold, that's why
they invented jackets.

Luckily

I'm also related to Mom,
who grew up in Colorado,
learned to ski young,
and says snow is cold vanilla
frosting on the mountaintops.

She drove Will and me
all the way from Las Vegas
to Mammoth Mountain,
paid for passes, equipment,
two beginner lessons for me.

Will had been there with her
a few times before, and like
everything sports, he had a real
talent for snowboarding.
He made it look easy.

It wasn't. I thought it would
be just like skateboarding.
It is, sort of, but it's different,
too. Just figuring out
the boots and bindings
took a while.

> *That's what lessons
> are for,* Mom said.

When I finished them,
I could pretty much make it
down the easiest runs
without falling.

Will volunteered
to stick with me
and offer a few tips
while Mom skied.

Once he knew
I'd nailed the basics,
he took a few harder runs
on his own.

But he kept checking
in, making sure
I didn't nose-dive
into a drift or surf
off beginner slopes
into the rough parts.
Will watched out for me.

Now
I have to
watch out for him.

Last Christmas, I asked
Mom if maybe we could spend
a day out on the mountain
before winter was over.
Her eyes went all sad
and her shoulders sagged.

I wish we could.
But what about Will?

See, Will Used to Play Football

He started in Pop Warner
when I still wore diapers,
not that I remember
way back then, but
I heard about it
plenty of times.

        It was one of the things
        our parents argued about.

Not the diapers.
At least,
I don't think so.
        But definitely the football.

Mom worried
about injuries.

        Dad insisted
        they were rare
        and every kid
        needed a sport.

Mom reminded
him Will bladed
and boarded.

        Dad said he meant
        team sports.

Mom and Dad argued
a lot before she left.
That time, Dad won.
I wonder if he's sorry now.

Will played
every game
every season.

He was good.
                Quick.
                        Sure-handed.
                                Fearless.

A reliable receiver
who could pull double
duty as a defensive end.

That made him a target.

Over the years,
Will took a lot of hits.
Most of them didn't seem
like much. Still,

> *A small bump here,*
> *a little bang there.*
> *Those can add up,*
> his doctor said.

But it was the big one
that knocked him out
of the game forever.

If I could just fix that,
everything would be okay.
But I can't. It's unfixable.

I'll Never Forget It

And neither will anyone else
who was there that night.

It was the last JV game
of the season, and Will wanted
to impress the varsity coaches
who were scouting for talent.
I remember how proud I felt,
watching him in his dark
green-and-gold uniform.

Mom was in the crowded
stands with Dad and me,
which was unusual.
She'd already left us by then.

Maybe not officially,
but she was on the road
singing lead and playing guitar
with her band a lot of the time.

Obviously, she didn't go
to many games. But that one
was important to Will,
and she happened to be
in town, so she came along.

It was the beginning
of the fourth quarter.
We were ahead, 14–7,
and Will had scored one
of our touchdowns.

So when he got the ball
again on the thirty-yard line,
the other team wasn't about
to let him run with it.

It was hard to see
what happened.

But even above the cheering,
it was easy to hear.

                              Hit from the back.
Hit from the front.

                    Will's helmet smashed

into a defensive guy's helmet.

                It sounded like a car crash.

As the two crumpled
to the ground, the cheering
stopped, replaced by
                              gasps
                              moans
                              a chorus of *no*s
                              a wail in my ear
that turned out to be Mom.

Players froze on the field.
Coaches and refs ran
to assess the wreckage.

At least one somebody
called 911.

Mom jumped up, but Dad
held her back.

              No. Wait. We'd just be
              in the way. He'll be okay.

She grabbed my hand,
kept repeating Dad's
words: *He'll be okay.*   *He'll be okay.*

We believed it because
in that moment, we had to.

        Sirens.
                Paramedics.
                        Gurneys.

Through it all,
Will and one defensive
dude lay very still.

I watched warm clouds
of breath hang
in the cold November air,
thinking how weird
it was for a crowd that big

              to be almost silent.

I Don't Know

What happened
to the other guy,
but what happened
to Will turned our lives

upside down.

Okay, look.
I get it that this isn't all about me.
I've heard that at least
a thousand times in the seventeen
months since Will's "incident."

That's what they call it,
because it wasn't exactly
an accident, even if
it wasn't exactly on purpose.
Will was knocked out,
and he stayed that way for hours.

At the hospital, we didn't hear
much for a long time
while the doctors tried
to figure out what was wrong.

Mom was a basket case.
I don't think she sat once
the whole time. Mostly
she wandered the hallways.
Anytime Dad tried to make
her chill, she'd shoot an evil glare.

Even without words,
her message to Dad was clear:

This is all your fault.

That wasn't fair.
But when you're scared,
blame comes easily.

We waited. And waited.
Guess that's why
they call them waiting rooms.
That one was painted pale
orange, like an unripe peach.
But it didn't smell like peaches.

It smelled like floor cleaner
mixed with B.O. mixed
with a faint stink of cigarettes,
like someone sweated smoke.

My mouth filled with
a taste like vinegar.
It was the flavor of fear.

The TV droned.
Dad stared at the screen.
Don't think he watched.
Mom paced the tile.
I played games on her phone
until I dozed off.

Heavy-Duty Whispering

Woke me up.
At first, I only caught pieces.

>   . . . *coma*
>   . . . *swelling*
>   . . . *brain injury*
>   . . . *nerve damage*
>   . . . *paralysis*

Luckily, that last one
came after the word "no."
All those sentence
fragments added up to this:

Will wasn't dead.
His arms still worked.
And so did his legs.
But his brain had volleyed
between the sides of his skull
so hard, it was swollen.
He was in a coma—that means
knocked out—but on purpose.
The doctor explained:

> *With a brain injury, some regions*
> *don't get enough blood flow.*
> *By keeping him asleep, those*
> *areas require less blood circulation.*
> *As the organ heals and the swelling*
> *goes down, there will be less damage.*

He Gave Will Drugs

To keep him deep asleep
for a couple of days.

Some brain injuries are easy
to spot. Others, not so much.

When it was safe for him to wake
up, we found out about both kinds.

The first was a thing called
cranial nerve damage.

Your cranium is your skull.
Under it is your brain.

On the bottom of your brain
are twelve pairs of nerves.

Some are connected to organs,
like your heart and lungs.

Others send info that helps you see,
hear, smell, taste, and feel pain.

Still others control muscles
that let you stick out your tongue,

turn your head from side to side,
and make your face show emotion.

Imagine

If you couldn't

smile   frown

pout
sneer

lift your eyebrows
scrunch your nose

jut your jaw

Kinda like your face
was frozen

except

for the obvious tic
that twitched one
cheek regularly.

Well, that's what can
happen when your
facial nerve is wrecked.

I'd say to ask Will,
but that isn't a great idea.
Because the second kind
of brain injury—the one
you can't always see—
lights his anger on fire.

I Mean, I Get It

Will's afraid to do all the things
he used to love. No more
                    football
                    skateboarding
                    snowboarding
                    mountain biking
because another blow
to his head could cause
worse damage.

That makes sense.
But he doesn't even watch
sports on TV anymore.
We used to do that together.

Mom wasn't much into
them, but Dad passed out popcorn
and soda like we were sitting
in the stands, watching in real time.

Baseball.
Football.
Basketball.
Soccer.
And skiing/boarding, of course.

The Winter Olympics
were, like, sacred.
Even Dad would plop down
in his chair and cheer.
TV snow isn't cold.

I miss stuff like that so much.
And other simple things,
like playing video games
together. Or board games.
Or trading comic books.

Will gave me my first
Lego Boost robot kit.
It was the coolest thing
ever. Not just the kit,
but how he helped me build it.

Probably what I miss
most of all, though,
is having a big brother
to talk to. Some things
you can't tell just anyone.

Like how mad you are
at your mom for walking
away when things got hard.

Like how when she left
she slit a hole in your heart,
and it bled a lot of love.

Like how you spend
way too much time hoping
something—anything—will
bring your mom home.

Will Would Understand

If he'd kept that door open,
but he slammed it shut,
and it wasn't the only one.
In ninth grade, he fell in love
with this girl named Skye,
and man, were they close.

When Will was in the hospital,
she visited almost every day.
And when he came home,
she was there for him.
Until one day when his depression
kicked into high gear.

I was in the kitchen,
but couldn't miss hearing.

> *Look at me!* Will yelled. *Look
> at my face! I'm a freak!*

She mumbled something
in a low, low voice.

> *How could you—how could
> anyone—love someone like me?
> No! Go away. Leave me alone.*

> Her voice rose then.
> *Stop feeling sorry for yourself.
> You're going to get better.
> I want to be here for you.*

Eavesdropping Is Bad

But I couldn't help it.
I sneaked into the hall,
where I could hear better.

Skye was crying. *I love you,*
Will. What kind of a person
would I be if I stopped caring
about you because of this?

A smart person. Skye.
You are beautiful. Perfect.
You deserve better than me.

She tried to reason with him,
but he stopped listening.

Stopped talking.

Finally, he left her sitting
on the couch, went into
his bedroom.

Closed the door.

If he noticed me standing
there, he acted like he didn't.

I wasn't sure how
to make Skye feel better,
but thought I should try.
I liked her a lot.

Her eyes were dripping
into the palms of her hands.

When I reached out and nudged
her shoulder, she jumped
hard enough to spill brass-blond
hair from her loose ponytail.

　　　　Oh. It's you, she snapped.
　　　　You shouldn't sneak up on people.

"Sorry. Didn't mean to scare you."

　　　　She wilted. *It's okay. I'm fine.*

"I get that you're upset. But I bet
he'll change his mind. Mom
says he needs time to adjust."

　　　　Like, how much time?
　　　　It's been almost two months.
　　　　All I want is to help him.

"He's stubborn, you know.
But he'll come around."
We agreed he probably would,
and I walked Skye to the door.

She hasn't been here
in the fifteen months since.

And Will still hasn't come around.

I Wish I'd Fixed That

I tried. I did. But I only
made everything worse.
Not just between Skye and Will.
Between him and me, too.

A few days after their argument,
he was sulking around,
griping about not being able
to go anywhere. He still
hadn't been cleared to drive.

His doctor was working
to find the right combo
of medications to fight

                his depression
                his anxiety
                his pain
                his muscle spasms
                his aggression

all because of his messed-up
brain. Regulating it
wasn't going to be easy.

I hated to see him wrestle
with that, so I said,
"Maybe you should call Skye.
She always makes you feel better."

His Anti-Aggression Pill Wasn't Working

What do you know about Skye
and me? She and I are none
of your business, anyway.

His fingers folded into fists
and I really thought he might
come after me.

"Hey, Will? I'm just trying
to make you feel happier.
I don't know how to—"

> *Don't you get it? You can't*
> *make me happy. And neither*
> *can Skye, or anyone else.*

"Not even if I do your homework?"
Joking with Will always made
him smile. Except not anymore.

> *You're just a dumb kid!*
> *How could you do my homework?*

Dumb. That stung, because
I always thought my big
brother respected how hard
I worked to get straight A's.

It was the first time
I saw he didn't care.

I Don't Joke With Will

Very much anymore.
Sometimes a funny slips out.
Sometimes he even laughs.
But mostly he acts like I'm invisible.
Even when we're together,
which isn't so very often.

He drives me to and from
school, and sometimes
to Little League practice.

But he only goes to games
once in a while, and when he does
he pretty much keeps his face
glued to his phone. He used
to cheer for me. Of course,
once upon a time, so did Mom.

I remember waiting to bat
and seeing them together
in the stands. They looked
so much alike, with sun-
toasted skin and black hair,
hers cut almost as short as his.

And if I got a hit or caught
a fly ball, they'd jump to their feet
and yell some combination of:

> *Way to go, Trace!*
> *Woo-hoo! Woo-hoo!*
> *That's how to do it!*

But Now Nothing's the Same

I keep thinking if I
        stay cool
        wait patiently
        cause no problems

Will's brain will
unscramble itself.

I keep thinking if I
        take up the slack
        make things easier
        don't push too hard

my brother will want
to hang out with me again.

I keep thinking if I
        keep his secrets
        don't tell Dad
        don't bother Mom

he'll trust me enough
to tell me why he hardly
ever leaves his room
when he's home, and where
he goes when he ducks
out the door the minute
Dad's back is turned.

I miss the original Will.
I bet his old friends miss him, too.

Will Has New Friends

I mean, I guess that's what
you could say they are.
Not sure they actually
enjoy each other's company.

Not like the guys Will
used to hang out with.
They used to joke and talk
about girls and watch
games on TV.

These dudes look tough.
Not football kind of tough.
Rough kind of tough.

Mom would probably call
them a bad crowd.
But Mom's never around.
Yeah, she was gone a lot
before Will's incident.
But after, her music gigs
lasted longer and longer.

One day she went off with
her band and never came
back, at least not to stay.

I think it's half because
she can't forgive Dad and
half because she can't forgive
herself. She can barely look at Will.

And Dad? Most of the time
he's working, or chilling
after his casino shifts.

Usually we see him
at breakfast. Sometimes
before we go to bed at night.

Which mostly leaves Will
and me on our own.

Which mostly leaves
me on my own.

Not sure where Will goes
when he leaves with his new
buddies. I have no clue
what they might do.

But I'm almost positive
they don't watch sports.

They might talk about girls,
but I bet what they say
isn't very nice. I just hope
Will stays out of trouble.

Seems to me
he's looking to find it,
and there's plenty around
on the streets of Las Vegas,
especially right now.

It's Spring Break

People always come to Vegas
to party, but April is crazy.

Not only are people out
of school, but the weather
is hot, not blistering.

I've heard about kids
even younger than Will
bumming beer and cigarettes
from tourists. Will's new crowd
seems like those kind of people.
I worry about what he does
when he's with them.

As for me, I'd rather get attention
by doing regular stuff well,
like acing report cards and
building my Little League
batting average. I'm a pretty
good hitter, a decent pitcher,
and not bad at first base.

That's where I'm heading now.
I can ride my bike to practice,
which is good since there's no
one here to drive me.

I'm grabbing my glove
when Dad calls.

You up for burgers after work?

"Sure!" We hardly ever go out
to dinner on days Dad works.
He doesn't get off until eight,
which makes dinner pretty late
on school nights.

But hey, it's spring break!

"Where do you want to go?"

I was thinking Steak 'n Shake.

Their burgers are amazing,
but it's clear across town.
"Are you going to pick me up?"

I hadn't planned on it. Why?

"Too far for me to ride my bike."

He pauses. *What about Will?*
He can drive you, can't he?

He's supposed to be transportation
when I need it. That's why Dad
bought him his clunker.

"Um. He isn't here, and I'm not
sure when he'll be back."

This Pause Is Longer

I think I blew it.
Is Will gonna be mad
I said something?
Probably, I'm guessing.

Finally, *Where did he go?*

"He said he was meeting
friends at the arcade."

What arcade?

"I don't know."

How long has he been gone?

"A couple of hours."
Longer, but I won't say so.

*Not okay. He's supposed
to be taking care of you.*

I can picture Dad's face,
all red and puffed up. Mad.

"It's okay, Dad. I'm twelve,
I can take care of myself,
and I was just heading out
to practice anyway.
I always ride my bike there."

*He takes a deep breath.
You're a good kid, Trace.*

"You're a good dad, Dad."
I mean it. He isn't perfect,
but he tries really hard
to take decent care of us.

> Thanks, son. Listen. If Will
> isn't back by the time you get
> home from practice, I'll put
> you in an Uber or something.
> It's Steak 'n Shake or bust.

"Yay!"

> In fact, bring a friend if you
> like. Make it a sleepover.

"Really? Awesome."

> Okay. My break's over. Text
> me if you need that ride.

"Bye, Dad."

What got into him? I haven't
had a friend spend the night
in a while. Something's up.

No Time

To think about that now.
My coaches don't appreciate
when we're late
for practice.

I strap my glove and bat
to my bike, jump on,
pedal hard.

Feel the burn,
some people say.
I can, and what that means
is the lunch calories
my body's burning are turning
into kinetic energy—
the energy of motion.
That's what moves the bike.

I'm kind of a STEM geek.
Formulas and equations
make sense to me
because the rules
stay the same.

They don't have minds
that can change,
like people do.

Math and science
are important elements
of so many different things.

Music, for one.
There's math in the patterns
that make songs, science
in the way sound waves move.
When I play my keyboard,
it's sort of like solving equations.

Sports? All of them rely
on math and science,
especially physics.

Take baseball.
Pitching, fielding,
batting, running, sliding.
Natural forces come
into play.

Energy.
Motion.
Friction.
Drag.
Momentum.
Gravity.

Understanding how
they interact can make
you a better player.

So, yeah, I've studied
up a little. Okay, maybe
more like a lot.

Pedaling My Bike

As hard as I can,
I zip by our next-door neighbor
Mr. Cobb, who lets me
mow his lawn and pull weeds
to earn spending money.

He's a funny old guy,
but kind of nosy. Like,
he's always got gossip
to tell while he hangs out,
"monitoring my progress."

Mr. Cobb waves like he wants
to talk to me, so I yell,
"I'm late!" If I stopped,
practice would be half over
by the time I got there.

I make it just as Coach Hal
calls us to the batting cages.
Before we line up, he makes us sit.

*I want you all to welcome
our newest player, who just
transferred from Santa Monica.
Say hi to Catalina Sánchez, everyone.*

Catalina? A girl? On our team?
Girls don't even play
ball with us at school.
I'm not the only one who groans.

Coach Hal won't have it.
Seriously? Maybe you all
need to run a few laps.

It's okay. Her voice is cool,
not even a little upset.
I'm used to it. But call me Cat.

All the guys look around.
She's sitting off to one side.
Why didn't I notice her before?

Maybe because,
with her long, dark
hair pulled back and
her wearing a team
uniform, she looks almost
just like the rest of us boys.

But looking like
and playing like
are different things.
Guess we'll see.

Okay. Let's get in some batting
practice. You go first, Cat.

She frowns. *Because I'm a girl?*

No. To show us what you've got.

Everyone Stares

As Cat steps into the cage, left
of the plate as right-handers do,
lifts her bat to her shoulder.

Her stance is good.
So is her focus.
And her swing is level.

First try, she boosts one
deep to the outfield.
Coach Tom pitches another.

She swings a little late,
but still manages to catch
wood. This one goes foul.

Three more pitches.
Three more hits.
She moves around the plate.

She bats left-handed, too?
No one in this division bats
from both sides, not that I've ever seen.

I nudge my buddy Bram.
"She thinks she's a switch-hitter."
On the first pitch, she proves it.

Bam! She hits that baby
straight over Coach Tom's
head and into right field.

Four more pitches.
A couple of ground outs.
The other two are solid hits.

What? No way! A girl!
And she's just as good batting
right-handed or left? Crazy!

*Coach must've gone easy
on her,* says Bram. *Maybe
you should pitch to her.*

"Yeah." I agree, but I have
a feeling it wouldn't make
a bit of difference. She's decent.

*Very impressive, Cat. You'll
make a great addition to the team.
Okay, who's going next?*

The rest of us take our turns
in the cage. The pressure to
outperform her is strong.

Too strong. Not one of us
succeeds. Not even just batting
from one side of the plate.

Coach Hal offers encouraging
words, but his grin keeps
stretching wider and wider.

He reminds me of a buff blond
teddy bear, because under all those
muscles and stern talk, he's gentle.

Cat doesn't smile or act
stuck-up. She stands, watching.
Bram and I wander over to her.

"Hey. I'm Trace Reynolds. How long
have you played Little League?
And who taught you to hit?"

She barely glances at me.
Started tee ball at four.
And my dad taught me.

Bram whistles. *Your dad sure*
knows his stuff. But why you?
Doesn't he have any sons?

Cat grits her teeth. *Dad played*
in the majors. He has two sons.
But he says I have the talent.

Bram Snorts

I laugh.
At the snort.
At Cat's answer.

What's so funny? she asks.

"You are. At least, I think so."

She could get mad. Doesn't.
Yeah, maybe I am. Dad says
it's one of my best qualities.

I want to know who her dad
is and what Major League
teams he played for, but Coach
Hal ends batting practice
to work on our fielding.

We all gawk at Cat,
who's kind of amazing
in the infield.

To start, she's fast, and her hands
are quick, scooping up
grounders and snatching flies.

As usual, Coach Tom,
who kind of specializes
in pitching, calls people
off the field two at a time
to throw and catch.

Not everybody gets a turn,
but not everyone wants one.

Pitching is hard.
Catching is worse.

I mean, watching a ball
flung toward your face,
you tense and hope it gets
really close, otherwise
you'll have to chase it,
which, in a game, could
mean someone scores.

Not where I want to play.
I like to pitch, and today
I get to practice first.
Miguel catches, and
together we look decent.

Okay! yells Coach Tom.
Switch out! Bram, you catch.
Cat, let us see your arm.

No switch-pitching, thank
goodness. There's a guy
in the majors who can throw
equally well with both arms,
which is totally weird.

But Cat only pitches right-handed.

I Might Be Better

But she isn't exactly bad.

She lifts her glove
and her left knee
at the same time,
achieving balance.

Now she reaches
for power, thrusting
that left leg toward the plate
as she brings her pitching
hand back and drives
her glove forward, building
a superstrong stance.

Propelled by a shove
from her right leg,
she rotates her arm
toward the target, and *zap!*
The pitch hits Bram's mitt.

Hard.

                    Nice! yells Coach Tom.
                    Let's see another one!

Cat repeats the process.
This one's a little low, and as
she tosses several more,
I can see that's how
she tends to throw.

When those kinds
of pitches pull away
from a batter,
they're really hard to hit.

A few   go high.
A few   go wide.

But Bram catches
every single one
without trying too hard,

and that is the mark
of a decent pitcher.
They make a good combo.

I can't help but watch,
mouth hanging open.

Half in awe.
        Half jealous.

How can a girl
have that kind of skill?

I'm So Busy

Thinking about that
I almost forget about
asking someone to spend
the night. I could invite
Lucas or Trevor or Antonio.

They're all buddies.

But Bram is my best
friend on the team.
He goes to my school
and was, like, the first kid
there to even say hi to me.

If I'm gonna share Steak 'n Shake
with someone, he's my first choice.

As Coach Hal calls us in
for the final pep talk, I ask
Bram, "Hey. Wanna get
burgers and stay over tonight?
Dad says it's cool."

    Sure, if the PUs say okay.

PUs is short for Parental Units.
That means his mom and dad.
Bram says weird stuff like that
all the time. That's one reason
I like him. He's entertaining.

Bram's PUs

Give permission.

In fact, his mom says
he can stay a whole week
so she can save money
on their grocery bill.

She's kind of entertaining, too.

We come up with a plan.
I'll ride my bike home.

She'll take Bram
to their house
so he can change out
of his uniform
and grab his toothbrush.

Then she'll drop him off.
Or, if Will isn't home, she'll drive
us to Steak 'n Shake to meet Dad.

After Coach Hal lets us go,
I hang out for a few,
hoping maybe I'll see
Cat's dad and figure out
who he is. But she gets
in a car with a lady.

Oh well. Maybe next time.

On the way home,
I don't have to pedal so hard.
Still, before too long
I'm sweating.

Even with the sun dropped
behind the mountains,
the desert air is like toast—
crispy hot and dry.

In the dead heat
of a Las Vegas summer,
bike riding only happens
in the early morning
or close to dark.

Or, if I'm really lucky
and Mom's around, she might
take me up into the nearby
hills for some hard-core
mountain biking.

Maybe next time she's here
she won't even ask
                    What about Will?

And if she does, maybe
for once I should ask back,
What about me?

Yeah, I Get It

That would make me
sound selfish.

But I'd have to work
really hard to be more
selfish than she is.

I love her lots.
I mean, she's my mom,
and loving her
kind of goes
with the job
of being her kid.

But how I feel
about her is . . .
complicated.

She was never mean
to Will and me.
Never hit us.
Never yelled.

But sometimes
she made me think
we were in her way.

Like there were so many
places she dreamed
about seeing, and things
she wanted to do.

Only, being our mom
made them impossible.

One time she was talking
about wanting to travel
to Paris, France.
"Can we all go?" I asked.

> *Oh, honey, no. It would
> be much too expensive.*

I don't think money
was the problem, though.
No, she wanted freedom.

She fronted her band,
Obsidian, before she met Dad,
doing a gig in the casino
where he worked.

That's how they got together.
That's how they fell in love.
That's how they got married.

While Mom was still happy
at home, Obsidian mostly
only played in Vegas,
but when she decided life
with us wasn't enough,
the band went on tour again.

Some People

Might not think
that's selfish.

But I do.

Mostly because
I miss her.

Sometimes I wake
up at night, sure
I can hear her singing.

But then, when I listen
real hard, all I can hear
is the wind outside.

Sometimes I come
home from school
and head straight
to the kitchen,
where she used to help
me with my homework.

But now, when I toss
my backpack onto
a chair, there's no one
there to ask about my day
or keep me from sticking
my fingers into the jar
of peanut butter.

Sometimes I unscrew
the lid from the bottle
of her shampoo I hid
in my closet, just to
remember how earthy
her hair always smells—
like rosemary and vanilla.

But then, when I close
it up, my room reeks
again of dirty socks
and stinky shoes
and I have to crack
a window or two.

Sometimes when I ride
my bike up the driveway,
I remember to put it in
the garage, leaning it on
the kickstand, safe
from front-yard thieves
or wayward cars.

Other times, like right
now, I totally don't care
and leave it dumped
sideways on the lawn.

When I think too hard
about Mom, I don't care
about anything.

Will Isn't Here

So I scoot around
the house, into the side
yard, and unlock the door
with the key we keep
stashed beneath
the garden gnome's butt.

The air inside hangs
like a hot blanket.
Dad makes us keep
the air conditioner low
when we're not home.

I crank it up now,
and as I reach
for the button,
a wicked stench
leaks from my armpit.

Better clean up
or they might not
let me inside
the restaurant.

First, I try to call Will
and see if he can give
us a ride. But it goes
straight to voice mail.

Big surprise.

I go to my room, grab
some clean clothes, dump
my uniform in the bathroom
hamper. Dad wants us to help
him keep things neat.

> *I have to work hard enough*
> *without picking up after*
> *the two of you boys.*

That's true, so why would
Will toss his dirty stuff on the floor
right next to the laundry basket?

I take care of that for him,
turn the shower to barely
lukewarm, step under
the not-quite-cool waterfall.
Ah! That feels good.

Good enough to make me
want to sing. I must've caught
the music bug from my mom.
I guess I sing
      way too loud
            way too much.

> *Tone it down, please,*
> Dad always says.

      Will just yells, *Shut up!*

But I Won't Bug Anyone

Singing here in the shower.

One of Mom's favorite songs
comes to mind, and as I lather
my hair, I belt out, "I'm still
standing. Yeah, yeah, yeah . . ."

A stream of shampoo
gets into my eyes.
I'm fighting the sting

      when suddenly
            something crashes,
                  really smashes,
                       in the house.

What do I do?
      Is it a burglar?
            Should I yell?
                 Be super quiet?

I'm still soapy when I turn
off the water, grab a towel,
and wrap it around me
before cracking the door
and peeking out.

Someone's in the house,
for sure. But who?
And how did they get in?

I hear feet crunching on
pieces of whatever fell.
The noise is coming from . . .
my room. At least, I think so.

My heart thumps.

Too fast.
        Too hard.

Feels like it might pop
right out of my chest.

I slide clothes over
my sticky skin.

Nudge the door open.
        Plot my escape.
                Get ready to run.

On your mark . . .
        get set . . .
                go!

I Sprint

Down the hall,
eyes on the front door.

But the bottoms
of my feet are still wet,
and all of a sudden
I'm skidding.
      Sliding.
            Slipping.

Just past my room,
down I go. "Ow!"
The word falls out
of my mouth,
and now I'm caught.

Sure enough,
footsteps slap
in my direction.

           Dude! You okay?

"Will! When did you get
home? And what are you
doing in my room?"

His face turns the color
of a tomato and he starts
to stutter.

        I—I—I . . .

And now I remember
the crashing noise.
I don't even stand up,
just crawl real fast,
trying to get into my room.

Will blocks me.

"What did you break?"

More sputtering. *I—I* . . .

Something goes off
inside me, sharp
and hot, like a

F
I
R
E
C
R
A
C
K
E
R
!!!

I Reverse a Little

Take aim, bomb straight
into his legs, knocking
him backward, but somehow
he stays on his feet.

>   *You little . . .*

Will's a lot bigger than me.
Thump! Oof! Thwack!
Ow—again!

Only, this time my chin
smacks the floor and I find
myself facedown, big brother
straddling my back. "Let. Me. Up."

>   *Not till you say you're sorry.*

The only part of me
I can move is my head,
and when I lift it, my eyes
travel across the hardwood
boards to the open closet door.

Just inside is a splash
of coins, and the peanut
butter jar that spilled them
when it fell off the shelf
where I keep it, filled
with my allowance and
odd-job cash I've earned.

There should be bills, too,
but I can't see any of them.
I force my voice steady.
"What happened to my money?"

The pressure on my back
vanishes as Will jumps up.
He's totally busted, so he has
nothing to say but the truth.

*I borrowed some. I'll pay
you back. Don't worry.*

"But you have your own money.
Why would you take mine?
What do you need it for?"

Something important, okay?

I want to know more, but
the look on his face tells me
I'd better let it drop.

"When will you pay me back?"

As soon as I can. I have to go.

"Dad's taking us to Steak 'n Shake.
You're coming, right?"

Can't. Not tonight.

Just Like That

He leaves.
No apology.
No see you later.
No asking if I need a ride.

If he was going to borrow
money, why didn't he ask?
Wait. Was he going to
straight-up steal it?

If I didn't find him there
in my room, right after
the peanut butter jar
crashed, I might never
have known where
that money went.

I'm not sure about
the change, but I'm positive
I had about sixty dollars
in ones, fives, and tens.

And now it's all gone.
Will took it.

What kind of brother
does something like that?

Will's been super hard
to get along with for a while.
But lately there's something else.

Something more.
Something worse.
Something strange.

Even after his injury,
even when he was distant,
he used to be decent.

Maybe he wouldn't talk
much, but stealing?
Cheating? Lying?

No, he did not do
those things.

I need to talk to Dad.
But it's hard when he's so busy.

I need to talk to Mom.
But she doesn't have time for me.

I need to put this family
back together.

I can.
I know it.
I can fix it.
I have to.
But I don't have
                a clue how.

I Call Bram

Tell him to let his mom know
we'll need that ride after all.

Then I text Dad, who's still
working his shift:

**Will isn't here, but Bram's mom
can drive us. Meet you at 8:15?**

It's a few minutes before
I get his text back:

> *Better make it 8:30. If I'm not
> there when you get there, I will be
> shortly. Mouth's watering already.*

Bram should be here around
eight. While I wait, I scoop up
the spilled coins, count as I put
them back in the jar. Twelve
dollars, sixty-two cents.

Guess I'd better keep a total
so I know if more goes missing.

I wonder why he needed the money.
It must've been important.
Besides, what happened to
his own stash of allowance cash?

And should I tell Dad?

I'm Still Thinking That Over

When Bram thunk-thunks
the door-knocker thing.

When I open up, he just stands
there. He leans forward, squints,
runs a hand through the blond
stubble covering his head.

What's wrong with your face?

"What's wrong with *your* face?"

*No, dude. I mean it. What
happened to your face?*

I'm confused. "Um . . . what?"

He pushes inside,
sets down his backpack.

*Your jaw is black and blue.
Did somebody punch you?*

I touch my cheeks. Chin.
Ouch. Now I remember.

"No, but Will knocked me
down. It's really that bad?"

Go look in the mirror.

He follows me to the bathroom.
I flip on the light, and . . . whoa!

Spreading right and left
from the cleft in the middle
of my chin is a huge bruise.

"Wow. That's beautiful, huh?
Think Dad will notice?"

>Unless he's mostly blind
>and can't find his glasses.
>Why did Will do that to you?

"Your mom's waiting.
I'll tell you in the car."

I lock the front door behind
us and we get in the back seat
of a sweet little Mustang.
Someday I want a car like this.
Or maybe a Ferrari.

Bram's mom says hi and
looks in her rearview mirror.

Before she can ask, I say,
"I know. What went down is . . ."

By the Time

We get to Steak 'n Shake,
they know all the details.

Well, except for
the details I don't know.

That's messed up, says Bram.

It's not my place to say, adds
his mom, *but you really should
talk to your father about it.*

"I know." I'm quiet for
a second. "Do you think
Will's in trouble?"

Sounds like he could be.

"Thanks, Mrs. Martin.
I'll definitely talk to Dad."

I will. But when?
Before, during, or after burgers?
Not to mention the fries.
Ooh, and a shake. Maybe Oreo—

So, we going in or what?
Bram sounds impatient.

"Sorry, man. Just call me
milkshake brain."

MB for short?

We agree that works
and head inside.

The hostess says we can
look for Dad, but I don't see
him yet, so Bram and I wait
in chairs against one
peach-colored wall.

I'm glad I'm not waiting
by myself, or I'd be bored.
Bram and I talk about baseball
and whether or not girls
should be able to play
on the same teams with guys.

Bram says no, but I ask,
"Well, what if a girl really
could play just as good?"

He shakes his head. *Maybe
in Little League. Would
never happen in the majors.*

"Probably not. But I'm
saying what—"

The door opens. In walks
Dad. He's not alone.

The Lady

Who's with him is pretty.
Not like a movie star.
Like a real person.

Natural.

I don't think she's wearing
makeup, and her hair falls
to her shoulders in thick
brown ribbons. Easy, like
all she has to do is brush it.

I notice that before Dad
spots me. When he does,
he lifts his hand to wave.

The lady's hand
      slips out of his,
            drops to her side.

Wait . . . what?

      Bram pokes me. *Who's that?*

"No clue."

She follows Dad over to
where we're sitting.

          Hey, boys, says Dad. *Good
          to see you again, Bram.*

It's pretty bright in here,
so Dad can't help but see
the dark bruise on my chin.

> *What happened to you?*
> *Did you get hit by a ball?*

I shake my head. But now
I don't want to talk about
Will. Not in front of a stranger.
"I tripped and bumped the floor."

Bram gives me one of those
looks that means *seriously?*
But he doesn't say anything.

> *You should be more careful,*
> says Dad. *You don't want*
> *to knock out a tooth or something.*

"Right." I stare at the lady,
who clears her throat,
waiting for an introduction.

> *Oh!* The tips of Dad's ears turn
> red, and I bet they feel hot.
> *This is my friend Lily. Lily, this*
> *is Trace and his buddy Bram.*

Lily Smiles

It makes her face
look really friendly
and I don't want it to,
because she isn't my friend.

But she is Dad's friend.
What does that even mean?

So good to meet you, Trace.
Your father brags about you
so much I feel like I know you.

"Interesting. He hasn't
even mentioned you."

Cold.
Frosty.
Like how I feel inside.

Trace—

It's okay, Sebastian. I'm sure
this came as a huge surprise.
Let's get a table. I'm starving.

Huh. I think I just lost
my appetite. I'm not
a big fan of surprises.

At least, not this kind.

No One Says Much

As we're seated near
the back of the room.

Lily and Dad discuss the menu,
but Bram and I already know
what we want to order.

I must be hungry after all,
because the smell of burgers
sizzling on the grill and the sound
of fries crackling in vats of hot oil
make my mouth start to water.
Maybe it's noticeable, because
Lily is staring at me.

*Has anyone ever told you how
much you resemble your dad?*

Dad nods. *Trace got my Puerto
Rican good looks, that's for sure.*

Lily laughs, then asks,
And what about Will?

*He looks more like his mother.
Handsome, but French descent.*

I see, says Lily. *But where is he?
I was hoping to meet him, too.*

He never came home? asks Dad.

I Don't Want to Lie

"Well—"

Did you try to call him?

"His phone was off."

Bram elbows me in the ribs.
I grunt, but no one notices.

"Actually, Will came
home for a few minutes.
I told him about dinner
and asked for a ride.
He said he was busy."

Dad frowns so hard,
his eyebrows touch.
He knows there's more.

I worry about that boy.
He hardly ever talks to me.
Seems like all he does is sulk,
when he's not blowing up.

What about therapy? asks Lily.

He went regularly for a while,
but now he refuses. I've asked
him to give it another try, but
he says it's a waste of time.

A waitress comes over
to take our order, and
I'm happy she interrupts.
I don't want to talk about
Will with a stranger.

But it's Lily who changes
the subject.

Tell me about school, Trace.
I hear you're super bright.

GATE. That's gifted and talented!
And he gets all A's, too.

Dad actually sounds
proud of me. Weird.
Guess I can talk about
Rainbow Ridge. It's a K–12
public charter school.
Will and I both go there.

In fact, we moved
to our neighborhood
to be closer and make
it easier. Dad said it was so
Will could keep an eye
on me, but I know it was
the other way around.

Not that we see each
other much at Rainbow.

I'm on the lower campus,
but it's attached to the upper,
where middle and high schoolers go.

I tell some of that to Lily
but don't mention I hated
leaving my old school and
friends behind, or anything
too personal. I still don't get
why I'm talking to her at all.

So when our milkshakes
land on the table, I take a big
slurp and ask, "Do you work
at the casino with Dad?"

> Dad shakes his head. *Lily's*
> *the recreation coordinator*
> *at the retirement village*
> *where my dear old dad lives.*

Grandpa Russ moved out here
from Minnesota after Grandma
Isabel passed away.
He didn't like the cold, either.
Said he only lived there
because that's where he grew up
and he didn't know better.

"That's how you met? Visiting Grandpa?"

It's a *Duh* Question

The kind you already know
the answer to, but you can't
stop your mouth from asking.

> *Well, sort of,* says Lily.
> *I was organizing—*

"Wait. Let me guess.
A shuffleboard tournament."

> She giggles. *No, though I am
> responsible for those, too,
> as well as golf, bridge, yoga,
> water aerobics, camping trips,
> movie nights, and ski weekends.*

I want to ask if lots of old
people ski, but Dad interrupts.

> *Lily was putting together
> a casino night, and my dad told
> her I might be a good connection.*

> *I was going to call, but happened
> to be downtown, so I decided
> to stop by and meet Sebastian
> in person. He was very helpful.*

Her hand floats down
on top of his, like a leaf
drifting onto the ground.

I expect him to pull away.
But their fingers lock together.

No.
No.
No.

She smiles.
Looks into his eyes.
Dad stares back.

No.
No.
No.

I'm about to say exactly
that—one two-letter
word, on auto repeat—
when the waitress
comes with our food.

So instead, when I open
my mouth, it's to ask Lily
to please pass the ketchup.

At least it makes her move
her hand, which I try to ignore
while we finish dinner.

Like Always

The burgers and fries are killer.
So much better than frozen
stuff tossed in the microwave—
three minutes to something
that sort of looks like real food.

Some kids have parents who
cook. I know, because some
of them are my friends, and
that includes Bram. His mom
could be a restaurant chef.

My mom? Serene Etienne
might be a killer singer,
but her scrambled eggs
were runny, and she always
burnt the toast. And Dad?

Once in a while, on his days
off, he gives it a try. Will and I
gag everything down, emphasis
on the "gag." Usually, he gets
takeout. Pizza or Chinese.

So when Lily says,

> *We should all have dinner*
> *at my house soon. I'm a darn*
> *good cook, if I do say so myself.*

my first thought is, *Sure!*
Then I remember who's talking.

Doesn't Matter

Because Dad's all in.

>*Great idea! It's been a long*
>*time since we've had decent*
>*home cooking, huh, Trace?*

"What do you mean? Your
grilled cheeses are primo."
If you like barely melted American
on grease-soaked white bread.

>*Yeah, sure. I see the way you*
>*and Will eat them—swallowing*
>*hunks with big gulps of juice.*

>>*I'm sure they're wonderful,*
>>*Lily says. But I was thinking*
>>*maybe enchiladas or carnitas.*
>>*You like Mexican food, don't you?*

>*I do!* says Bram.

>>*My favorite!* says Dad.
>>*Well, after Puerto Rican.*

Oh, man, she's making this
hard, because I cannot tell a lie.
So I'll just tone it down a little.

"Uh-huh. It's okay."

It's Hard

Not to like Lily.

She smiles a lot.
Has really good manners.
Listens when you talk.
Acts like she's interested.

Probably fake.
Why would she care
about what I have to say?

But even in the car,
when Dad drives her home,
she keeps asking questions.

So, you and Bram are teammates?
What positions do you play?
What's your favorite Major League
team? Ever been to a game?

When I tell her no,
she shakes her head.

Let's remedy that. My brother
lives in LA. He's a Dodgers fan
and has season tickets.

"No way! Seriously?"

Third-base line, behind
the Dodgers' dugout.

Cool! says Bram.

Yeah. Why does she have
to be so cool? Annoying.

Dad turns the car into one
of those neighborhoods
where the houses all look alike—
beige with dark brown trim—
and there's a palm tree in every yard.

Actually, it looks a lot like
our neighborhood, only those
houses are gray and navy blue.
Except for all the weird stuff
on the Strip (which is wild!),
Las Vegas isn't very creative.

When we get to Lily's,
Dad parks the car and walks
her to the front door.
She left the porch light on
and I can see a bunch of moths
swarming around the bulb.

Lily puts her key in the lock,
then turns to say goodbye.

Don't look, advises Bram.

Too late.

Dad Kisses Her

Not on her forehead.
Not on her cheek.
Straight up on her lips.

Not too long.
Not real hard.
But it means something.

Maybe not much.
Maybe too much.
Now I need to know.

Bram checks out my face.

>   *You okay, dude?*

"Sure," I lie.

>   *You didn't know, huh?*

"Know what?"

>   *That your dad has a girlfriend.*

The word hits like a torpedo.
Girlfriend.
One word.
A *girl friend*, two words,
might be okay, and until
right now I could pretend
that's what she was.

"No. I didn't know."

The sentence scratches
my throat. My eyes sting.
Why didn't Dad tell me?
Who springs something
like that on his kid?

I wait till he gets back in
the car and turns out
on the main drag before
asking, "So, is Lily
your girlfriend or what?"

He doesn't say anything
for a minute or two.

We've been seeing each other, yes.

"How long?"

*He shrugs. A couple of months,
give or take. She's nice, right?*

"Yeah, she's nice.
Yeah, I like her. But . . ."

But what?

"But what about Mom?"

Dad Takes a Deep Breath

Holds it, and my question,
inside for a long while.
Finally, he exhales.

> *Trace, your mom and I have*
> *been divorced for over a year.*
> *Even before that, we weren't*
> *really together. You know that.*

"Yeah, but . . . it just feels . . ."

Wrong.
But I'm not sure why.

Like something ended.
Even if it did a while ago.

Like there's no turning back.
Not that I thought we would.
Anyway, would turning back
make everything better?

Maybe yes.
Probably no.
It was Mom's decision
to leave. She wasn't happy.
Neither was Dad.

I just don't know why
things have to get
more complicated.

"What about Will, Dad?"

What about him . . . what?

"What if this pushes him
farther away?"

I'm not sure that's possible.

"You haven't given up
on him, have you?"

*Of course not! Never! He's my son,
and so are you. You are the most
important people in my life.*

"More important than Lily?"

What did I just tell you?

I glance over at Bram, who's staring
out the window, pretending his fingers
are stuck in his ears. I should be quiet.
Instead, my mouth just keeps going.

"But you're in love with her."

*He's quiet for a second.
Yes, I guess I am, which
doesn't mean I love you less.*

"You're not getting married, right?" Please no. Please no.

Not tonight, Trace. Not tonight.

It's Almost Eleven

By the time we get home.
Will's car isn't here, which,
of course, Dad notices.
He glances at his watch.

> *One hour until curfew.*
> *Wonder what he's up to.*

This would be the time
to tell him about my money.
Instead I just say, "No clue.
Can Bram and I stay up for a while?"

> *Okay,* says Dad. *You can*
> *have until curfew, too, okay?*

"Cool."

The midnight curfew is a county
law for kids under eighteen.
It's not really a house rule.

But I'm usually in bed
by ten unless a friend
sleeps over.

Bram and I play *Minecraft*
for an hour, then say good night
to Dad, who's stressing
because Will is still gone.

"You can have the bed," I tell
Bram. "I'll take the floor."

Eew, dude. I don't want to sleep
on your dirty sheets.

"Me neither. Let's both
sleep on the floor."

I get a couple of quilts
from the hall closet, fold them
so they're like sleeping bags.
One half goes under us.
The other half can go over
if we get cold, but for now,
it's way warm enough without.
We try to get comfortable.

Now Bram asks, *Why didn't you*
tell your dad about Will?

"After everything else,
it didn't seem so important."

Are you mad about Lily?

"Not really. It's just, Dad's
been 'too busy' for Will
and me, so how did he find
enough time to fall in love?"

The Question Floats

Like a feather in the darkness.
I don't expect an answer.
Not from Bram, for real,
because what he says is:

>*You want your dad to be
>happy, don't you?*

"Sure! But I don't want
him to get married again.
I don't want a stepmom.
I want my real mom back."

>*He thinks that over, then,
>Where does she live?*

"In hotel rooms, mostly,
I guess. She's on the road
a lot of the time."

>*She doesn't have a house?*

"No. When she isn't traveling,
she stays with Maureen and Paul."

>*Who's that?*

"Her mom and dad. They don't
like to be called Grandma and
Grandpa. They live in Denver."

How often do you get to see her?

"Not very. The last time
was right before Christmas."

He whistles real quietly.
That's almost four months.

"Yeah, I know."

Weird, but I think this
is the first time I've talked
to Bram about Mom.
She's like a secret
I hide inside. But why?

"Want to see something?"

Okay.

I grab the flashlight
I stashed by my pillow
in case of emergency.

Scoot
my butt
across
the floor.
Open
the closet
door.

Way in Back

Behind a stack of Lego boxes
is the bottle of my mom's shampoo
and a couple of magazines.

Bram doesn't need to know
what Mom smells like,
so I leave the shampoo behind.

"Here. Hold this."
I hand over the flashlight,
sit next to him.

I've looked at the articles
so many times, the magazines
open automatically
to the correct pages.

The first is an old *Las Vegas
Weekly*. The headline says:

SERENE ETIENNE AND OBSIDIAN
WANT TO ROCK YOUR WORLD

"That's my mom when
she was twenty-three,
when she first came to Vegas.
Obsidian is her band."

Wow. She was hot!

"Bram . . . ," I warn.

Well, she was.

In the picture she's wearing
leather pants and a studded vest.
Her black hair is spiked and
tipped blue, and her skin
is smooth. No sign of wrinkles.

Like, duh. She was young.

Next I open a *Rolling Stone*
magazine. "This was last year."
It's a short article about
a song Mom wrote finding
a ton of fans on YouTube.

ETIENNE BALLAD RESONATES

The photo is a close-up
of Mom singing into a mic.
Her hair is softer, longer,
with sparks of silver.
Little lines like spiderwebs
decorate the corners
of her mouth and eyes,
which seem to stare
at some faraway place.

She's still pretty.

No. She's beautiful.

I Put the Magazines Away

Stash the flashlight
beside my pillow again,
lie back beneath
a blanket of night.

Bram goes quiet,
and soon the way
his breathing sounds
tells me he's asleep.

I try, but my brain
is stuck thinking
about Mom.

Four months without
seeing her, and she's only
called a couple of times.

Once on Will's birthday.
Once on mine.

Does she ever think about us?

Does she keep the pictures
we send to her?

Does she ever look at them
and wish she was with us?

Where is she tonight?

I'm Slipping Toward Sleep

When suddenly
    doors slam
        feet pound
            voices yell.

I sit up so fast, I go
dizzy and have to wait
before I jump up
and crack the door.

Where have you been?

At a friend's house.

What friend is that?

No one you know.

What were you doing?

Just hanging out.

Curfew is midnight.

Not if you're driving.

Yeah, well, you're grounded.

*Whatever, Dad. Not like
you can stop me from leaving.*

I Slip Out

Into the hall, watch Will stomp
toward the front door.
Dad steps between.
He draws himself up tall,
thrusts his chest forward.

> *You do not have my permission*
> *to go anywhere. Do you understand?*

Will should shrink away
from Dad. Instead, he gets
right up in his red, puffing face.

> *How are you going to stop me?*
> *Knock me down and tie me up?*

> *If that's what it takes.*

Even from here I can see both
of their fists knotting, unknotting.
Will tries to go around Dad.
Dad pushes him. Not hard,
but enough to move him back.
Still, if Will happened to fall . . .

"Stop!" I yell. "What are you doing?
Somebody's gonna get hurt!"

Both of them freeze,
like they never even
considered the possibility.

Dad softens first.

> *Trace is right, son. I don't want*
> *to hurt you. Please listen.*
> *I'm worried about you.*

> *Will glares at him. Since when?*
> *Anyway, don't bother worrying*
> *about me. I'm doing just fine.*

I could argue with that.
And I probably should.
But maybe tonight will make
him think. Turn him around.

> *I hope that's true, Will.*
> *I don't tell you this enough,*
> *but I love you lots. If you're*
> *going through something—*

Will laughs.
Really loud.
Out of control.
Sounds crazy.

> *Seriously, Dad? I've been going*
> *through something for a while now,*
> *remember? Look. Everything's jake.*

Everything Is Not Jake

"Jake" means okay, and Will
is so not. He turns, clomps
up the hall past me, goes
into his room, slams the door.

Dad . . . what's the word?
Deflates, yeah, that's it.
Like a bike tire with a leak.
He looks at me with sad eyes.

>Thanks for stepping up, Trace.
>Go on back to bed now.

"Okay, Dad. See you
in the morning."

Unlike Will,
I close the door quietly
behind me, in case
Bram managed to sleep
through all of that.
He didn't.

>Your brother's messed up.
>If I talked to my dad like
>that, phew! Big trouble.

Not much to say but "Uh-huh."

Bram's quiet for a couple
of seconds, then he asks,

Maybe you should call
your mom and tell her
what's going on. Maybe
she'd have some good ideas.

"Yeah. I will. But she doesn't
ever answer, and doesn't call
back very often."

Leave a message anyway.
If she doesn't know
something's wrong, how
can she help make it better?

I don't reach out to her
very often. It hurts to be
ignored, and I figure if I bug
her too much, she won't want
to be my mom at all.

Bram goes back to sleep,
but I have a hard time,
mostly because a bright
yellow moon is beaming
through the window.
It's shining on Mom somewhere, too.

I get up to close the blinds
and happen to catch a glimpse
of Will's car, disappearing
down the block. He escaped.

Despite Tossing and Turning

So much last night
that I actually rolled
clear across the floor,
I wake up early, mostly
because Bram is snoring
into his pillow.

I find my phone quietly.
Just 'cause I'm awake
doesn't mean my friend
has to be, too. I check
the time. Six thirty-five.

I go to the window, crack
the blinds. Phew. Looks like
Will came home at some point.
His car's out front.

Bram's words from last
night drift into my brain.

. . . how can she help make it better?

Mom's probably asleep
wherever she is, but I go
ahead and text her, hoping
it doesn't bother her too much.

**Hey, Mom. Miss you. Hope
you're good. Will's acting
weird. I'm worried. Call me?**

I'm Not Sure

If Dad knows Will left again
last night. He doesn't say
anything at breakfast.
I don't mention it, either.

> What Dad does say is *Your*
> *next game is Saturday, right?*
> *Lily said she'd like to come,*
> *and it happens to be my day off.*

He can only make a few
of our games, and I'm happy
this is one. Even if Lily tags along.

"Yeah. It starts at five."

> Will wanders in. *What does?*

"Our Little League game."

When he's tired, like from
staying out way too late,
the tic in his cheek
goes into hyperdrive.
I wonder if it's painful.

Dad doesn't seem to notice.

> *You should come to the game,*
> he tells Will. *There's someone*
> *I want you to meet.*

That Sounds

Like a disaster waiting
to happen. At my game.
In front of my coaches,
teammates, and friends.

"That's all right," I say.
"Will doesn't care much
about baseball, Dad."

Both of them look at me,
wondering why I'd try
to convince Will to stay away.

> *What's the matter? asks Will.*
> *Afraid you'd be embarrassed?*

Well, yeah, but not for
the reason he thinks.
"I can hold my own. I'm one
of the best on our team."

> *We've got new competition,*
> *though, says Bram. A girl,*
> *and she's really good, too.*

> *Is that a fact? That right there*
> *might be a good reason to watch.*

I doubt he'll come. That's cool.
And he never even asked Dad
who he wanted him to meet.

Late Morning

Bram's mom picks him up.
Dad leaves for work.
Will waits for both,
then he takes off, too.

Which leaves
me,
myself,
and I.

The three of us
could watch TV
or play Xbox, but
Mom is on our mind, so we
decide to practice keyboard.

Mom mostly sticks to guitar,
but she can play piano.
Drums, too. She taught
Will the guitar, but since
he was five years older,
he was that far ahead.
Catching up would be hard.
I asked for a keyboard instead.

She gave one to me
for my sixth birthday,
showed me the basics.
I picked up more on my own.
Mom says I have a gift.

It's like my fingers know
what to do to make music
that sounds pretty good.

Right now they start playing
a keyboard-heavy song by
one of Mom's favorite bands:
Queen. Obsidian used to cover
this song sometimes. Mom
said she could never measure
up to Freddie Mercury's vocals,
but I thought she sounded awesome.

The song is called "Too Much Love
Will Kill You." It's about someone
who has a new love while still
loving whoever got left behind.

I know Mom still loves us.
That's in the mothers' rulebook,
right? But is there anything
in there about falling in love
with someone else after walking
away from your family?

Is that what happened to Mom?
Is that why she doesn't call?
Is that why she won't visit?

Is too much love her problem?
Or is it not enough?

I'm Halfway

Through the song when
my phone tells me someone's
calling. When I see who it is,
a piece of me scolds
the rest for not believing.

"Hi, Mom."

Hey, Trace. What's going on?

"Not much. It's spring break,
so no school or anything.
Mostly just baseball. Oh, and
when you called, I was playing—"

*Right, right. But what I meant
was, what's going on with Will?*

Oh. Yeah.

"Well, I think he's running with
a bad crowd. Staying out late.
Taking off without permission."

Oh, so it's not about his health?

"No. I mean, kind of.
He might get hurt, right?
Or he could get into trouble."

She should be concerned
about him, too. She's not.

> *I wouldn't worry too much.*
> *Most teenagers go through*
> *that stage. I know I did.*
> *You probably will, too.*

Nope. No way. "You don't
know me very well."

It hits me that I'm not sure
she knows me at all.
But it doesn't seem to bother
her, because she laughs.

> *We'll see. We'll see.*
> *In the meantime, keep*
> *on being you. You're the best.*

She Wants to Go

Sounds like she's signing off.
I want to keep her longer.

"Will still gets depressed,
too. Like, when he's home,
he mopes in his room
and hardly even talks
to Dad or me."

Is he taking his meds?

"I guess so."

He'll be fine, then.

"Okay. If you say so."

*I do. Anyway, you're too
young to worry about stuff
you can't do anything about.*

"Hey, Mom. Any chance you can
come visit sometime soon?
Maybe that would help Will."

*I'll do my best. Right now
I'm stuck in Colorado.
Doing a gig in Telluride.*

"Still snow on the ground?"

I'm getting a little skiing in,
if that's what you're asking.
Snow's slushy and my legs
are getting a bit old for spring
runs. But I'm not giving up yet.

Mom's legs aren't that old.
She's just trying to make me
feel better about not being
there on the mountain with her.

"Hey, Mom? Could Will and I
maybe come visit Maureen
and Paul in Denver this summer?
I mean, if you'll be there, too."

I think that could be arranged.
How long has it been since
you've seen them? Two years?

It was the summer before Will's
incident. "Yeah. Give or take."

We'll have to make plans.
Do some hiking or something.

"Sounds good. But, Mom?
Would you please call Will?
Maybe it would cheer him up."

Think so? Okay. Love you.

Don't Forget

That's what I tell her
before I hang up.
Please don't forget
about Will.
And please don't let
him know it was my idea.

I go back to my keyboard,
but not to Queen.
Instead, I pound out a song
of my own, one with a hard,
driving beat. I call it "Guilt Trip."

I hope

        I made Mom feel guilty
        about not calling more often.

I hope

        she follows through,
        and the next thing she does
        is dial Will's number.

I hope

        she tells him he's on her mind,
        he's important to her, and
        most of all, that she loves him.

I hope.
I hope.
I hope.

Saturday Rolls Around

Hot and still, and I feel
lazy for most of the day.
I stay inside, reading
and playing video games.

With Will.

For whatever reason,
he's been okay the past
couple of days. Not reliably
here. Not always nice
when he was, but more like
the brother I used to rely on.

Maybe Mom did call him.
Maybe that's why.
But if I ask, he'll know
it was my idea, and that
would ruin everything,
so I stay quiet.

Right now I'm sitting
at the kitchen table
while Will fixes a late lunch.
He comes over, sets a huge
sandwich down in front of me.

Better ingest a few extra pregame
calories, especially if you want
to play better than a girl.

My cheeks go all hot.

He laughs. *Just teasing.*
Don't freak out.

"I'm not." That might be a lie.

At least he remembered.
I was sure he'd forget.
"Are you coming to the game?"

I was thinking about it.
You have any idea who
Dad wants me to meet?

Probably better to tell him
up front than to let it be
a surprise. I nod. "Lily."

Lily? Who's that?

"Apparently, his girlfriend.
Pretty sure he's at
her house right now."

He took off a couple of hours ago.

I hold my breath,
waiting
for Will
to explode.

But Nope

Oh. That's cool.

"I thought you'd be mad."

Why? He works hard.
He deserves a little fun.

My jaw drops.
I'm, like, stunned.

What's wrong?

"Don't you think it's messed
up that he can make time for
a girlfriend, but us, not so much?"

Will's mouth trembles.
If his face worked right,
that would be a huge grin.

Nope. In fact, if he's busy with her,
that means less chance of him
sticking his nose in my business.

Oh. Right.
I get it now.
He doesn't care
about Dad. Or me.

Will is only worried
about himself.

And So

I'm surprised
when he actually decides
to come to my game.
In fact, he drives me.

Last weekend of spring break
and people are everywhere.

The sidewalks are crowded.
The bike paths are crowded.
The parks are crowded.

I bet the pools and lakes
are crowded, too.

"Hey, Will? Remember
that spring break when
we camped at Lake Mead?"

>He nods. *It was critical that year.*
>*Hot, I mean. We stayed in*
>*the water most of the time.*

"And we had 'hold your breath
as long as you can' contests."

>*That's right. We did.*

"You won all of them."

>*Yeah, but you kept trying.*

"Can you still hold your
breath for a long time?"

*I don't know. I haven't tried.
Why? He sounds irritated.*

I shrug. "Sometimes I wonder
about how much you changed.
Like, how your body works
and stuff. Is that bad?"

What difference does it make?

"I'm just interested."

What do you want to know?

"Well . . . um . . . does
your head hurt?"

*Not most of the time, but
I do get hellacious headaches.*

"What about your face,
like when you try to smile?"

*Does that hurt? No, but
it's totally frustrating.*

"That could still get
better, though, right?"

He's Quiet So Long

I wonder if he's zoned out.
I guess he has, in a way,
working on what to say.

> *Anything's possible, Trace.*
> *That's what my doctors say.*
> *Sure. It's possible alien mystics*
> *will visit Earth and heal the planet,*
> *including me. But I doubt it.*

"Well, I'm going with
your doctors. I know it
will. I believe it will."

> *You still believe in Santa, too.*

"I. Do. Not."

Wait, that was a joke.

"I don't believe in Santa,
Will, but I do believe
in you."

> *Good luck with that.*

We both fall silent.
But I don't want this
conversation to end.
It's the best one we've had in . . .
forever.

Mostly Because

It's the only one
we've had in, like,
                    forever.

So I ask, "Hey, Will?
What do you believe in?"

                    Dumb question.

"No it's not."

                    He sighs. *I believe in facts,*
                    the stone-cold truth.
                    Not hypotheticals, fantasies,
                    maybes, or what I'd prefer.

                    I believe in what I see
                    in the mirror, in what
                    that means to my future.
                    I believe what I hear
                    when people say cruel things.

                    I believe my life will be short,
                    so why not live epically today?

I try to let all that sink in.
"Will, are you okay?"

                    Depends on the moment.

I wanted to feel better. I don't.

We Arrive

At my game a half hour
early for warm-ups.

Will goes to find
a shady place on the grass
while I play some catch
and do stretches.

Coach Hal calls us over
to give us the starting lineup.
I'm pitching.
       Bram's catching.
              Cat's on first base.

The Padres (that's us!)
are the home team,
so we take our places
on the field while
the Tigers get ready to bat.

From the mound,
I can see where Will's sitting,
looking at his phone.
But by the time I throw
the first pitch, Dad and Lily
still haven't shown up.

So they miss watching me

      strike out one batter
      pitch another into a pop-up out

put a guy on base
force their best batter into a ground out.

That's pretty good,
if I say so myself.

Coach Tom agrees. *Super-
duper pitching, Trace!*

Super-duper. Yeesh.

Now it's our turn to bat.
I notice Will's still alone,
and when he sees me look
his way, he shoots a thumbs-up.
Guess he was paying attention.
I wish he would more often.

Dad and Lily miss watching
our entire batting order.

Shawn strikes out.
Bram walks to first.
I get a decent base hit.

That puts me on first,
moves Bram to second.
And batting cleanup . . .

Cat Comes to the Plate

The crowd of parents
and kids goes kind of quiet,
like they didn't notice
our team had a girl
playing first base.

But the Tigers' dugout
starts to buzz about
our new player.

Some gasp.
Some laugh.
One or two make
mean comments.

She ignores it all.
Decides to bat left-handed.
That might be a mistake,
because she seems a little
off her stride.

      Takes a strike.
      Hits a couple of foul balls.
      Pops one up, but the catcher misses.

"You got this, Cat," I call.

She nods.
Steps back into
the batter's box.

I've got a good feeling,
so I take a decent lead.
Bram does, too.
And . . .

She slaps one over
the second baseman's head.
It drops for a base hit.
Maybe even a double.

Bram runs.
I run.
Cat runs behind us.

People cheer.
People yell.
Coach Hal swings his arms,
telling us to keep on running
and don't look back.

Bram scores.
I score.
Cat's tagged out at third base.

But we're ahead, 2–0.

Dad and Lily missed
every minute of it.

They Finally Show

Halfway through my second-
inning pitching match.
I'm doing okay.

One guy out.
One guy on base.
One guy at the plate.

It's full count—
three balls, two strikes.
One more strike, he's out.
One more ball, I walk him.

That makes me nervous.
I concentrate too hard.
Take too long to wind up.
He calls time-out, steps
away from the plate.

I take a couple of deep breaths,
but happen to glance toward
Will just as Dad and Lily
set up a couple of folding
chairs beside him.

Dad says something,
Will jumps up, smiling,
puts out his hand for Lily
to shake, and Dad claps
him on the shoulder.

Now my attention is there,
watching them instead
of the Tigers' batter.

Trace! yells Coach Tom. *Focus!*

I try. But I throw ball four
and the batter walks.
So now there are runners
on first and second.

I close my eyes, lecture
myself. "Dad hardly
ever comes to games.
Make him proud of you."

It works.
I strike out the next batter.
Two down, one to go.
I can hear Dad cheer,
and look over that way
as the next Tiger lifts his bat.

I see Dad take some money
out of his wallet, hand it
to Will. No, Dad, no. And now
Lily reaches into her purse.
No way! Not her, too!

Trace! shouts Coach Tom.

I Pitch

Without thinking.
Without aiming.
Without a solid windup.

CRACK!

The ball whizzes
             past my head.
                          I'm too slow to react.

Everyone's yelling.
                    Running.
                          Throwing.
                                    Sliding.
One Tiger scores.
Another one scores.
The one who hit winds up
on third, with a triple.

It's 2–2.

And it would be up to me
to try to keep it that way
with some decent pitching,
except Coach Tom walks
out to the mound.

Sorry, Trace. You seem a little
distracted. We're bringing in Cat.
You take her place on first.

He waves and Cat trots over.
Face hot, I hand her the ball.
She's pitching now. That's fine.
I just hope I can scoop up
grounders and handle fly balls.

Cat throws well. The guy on third
scores, but that's on me, and
she gets us out of the inning
only one run behind.

As we go to the dugout,
I chance looking at Dad, who
smiles and waves, pretending
I didn't mess up royally.

Will, I see, is gone.

The rest of the game, I play
okay, my teammates play better,
and by the time it's all over,
we manage to win, 5–4.

Coach Hal calls us over
for the postgame pep talk.

> *Way to go! You guys rock!*
> *Couple of flubs, but nobody's*
> *perfect. Go celebrate a game*
> *well played. I'll see you at practice.*

As Everyone Leaves

Head down, eyes on the ground,
I shuffle over to where
my coaches are standing
together, talking.

"Sorry I messed up."

> *Everyone has off days,*
> says Coach Tom.

> Coach Hal nods. *Just a couple*
> *of bad pitches. You hit well.*

"Glad I did something right.
My dad is here for once."

> *That's what broke your*
> *concentration, I bet.*

> *And you collected yourself*
> *after. That's important.*

Okay, I feel a little better.
"Thanks, Coaches. See you later."

When I turn, Cat is a couple feet
away. I think she's waiting for me.
Probably wants to rub it in.

> But no. She says, *Good game.*

"Coulda been better. But thanks.
You were pretty good, too."

You want to meet my dad?
He's right over there.

I look where she's pointing.
"No way! Your dad is Victor
Sánchez?" I'd recognize him
anywhere. "He's awesome!"

I happen to think so. He was
a decent third baseman, too.
So, you want to say hi?

"Heck yeah! Too bad Will left.
He used to be a big Dodgers fan."

Who's Will?

"My brother."

He's not a fan anymore?

"No. He says sports are boring."

Why?

"It's kind of a long story."

Cat's Cool

But I barely know her.

I'm not ready to talk
about Will with her.

I don't talk about him
with very many people.

Dad. Mom. Bram.
That's about it.

But she's waiting,
obviously curious.

So I say, "I think it's just
his new crowd, really.
They're not the sports type."

That's too bad.

"Yeah. It is. But I am.
Think your dad would
give me his autograph?"

Pretty sure he'd be happy to.

What will I have him sign?
A baseball? My gear bag?

Hey, I know. My glove!

Cat's Dad

Is, like, famous. At least,
if you follow baseball.
He was a superstar third
baseman before he retired
after last season.

"Be right back!" I tell Cat.

I run to inform Dad I'm about
to meet one of my sports
heroes. I can't believe it!
And neither can Dad.

Think it would be okay
for us to come, too?

"I guess." But I don't wait
for Lily and Dad, in case
Victor Sánchez is in a hurry.
Instead, I reverse course
and sprint over to where
he and Cat are waiting.

My stomach's doing backflips.
Victor Sánchez offers his hand
and mine shivers as I shake it.
"H-h-hi. I'm Trace."

Very nice to meet you, Trace.
You played a good game.

He watched.
He said I did good.
Oh, yeah.

"Th-thanks. I'm, like,
a really big fan. So is my dad.
Oh, this is my dad. And Lily."

They do the introduction
thing, then Dad says,

I didn't know you lived in Vegas.

We haven't been here long.
LA was becoming unlivable,
and I had no reason to stay.

Well, we're lucky to have you.
And you, too, young lady.
Looks like talent runs in the family.

Questions pop into my brain:

Why did they move *here*?
Why did they move *now*?

School will be out
in a few weeks,
so why not wait
until summer?

Too Many Puzzles

For one day.
At least now
I know who
her father is.

Before we break
this party up, I ask,
"Mr. Sánchez? Would
you please sign my glove?"

              Sure. Have a pen on you?

"Uh . . ."

Who carries a pen
to play baseball?

                    I do, says Lily, reaching
                    way down inside her bag.

I have to work hard
not to roll my eyes.
She would, of course.

Then again, I'm glad
she has one, because now
I own a guaranteed genuine
Victor Sánchez signed glove.
I'll keep it forever!

"Thanks! This is awesome."

I'll go get our chairs, says Dad.
Meet you two at the car.
See you again, Mr. Sánchez.

Victor. Please call me Victor.

First-name basis. Nice.
We head toward
the parking lot.

Lily chatters about
the weather and how
surprised she was that
Little League baseball
could be so exciting.

Victor (!) pretends
to be interested.

Cat and I fall back
behind them.

Finally, she asks, *Hey.*
What school do you go to?

"Rainbow Ridge."

She smiles. *Cool. That's where*
I'll be going, too. It will be
good to know somebody there.

What Are the Odds?

Only a couple of other
Padres players go to RRCS.

"How come you're not going
to some fancy private school?"

>Her dad hears my question.
>*Oh, we looked into them.*
>*But Cat was dead set against it.*

>*I went to one in LA the last*
>*couple of years. The teachers*
>*insisted on calling me Catalina,*
>*and all the girls talked about*
>*was boy bands and phones.*

>*And all Cat did was complain.*
>*We told her every school is different,*
>*and that includes private schools.*

>*Yeah, but I'd rather be just*
>*a regular kid. The kind that*
>*plays baseball and stuff.*

>*She's a good student, but loses*
>*interest in learning if she's unhappy.*

Valid. Wonder just how
good of a student she is.
Gifted and talented?
I'm betting probably.

Dad Takes Lily Home

But instead of dropping her off,
we go inside because she followed
through and we're having Mexican
food for dinner.

Her house looks small on the outside,
but the living room, dining room, and kitchen
are like one giant open space.

You can tell a lady lives here.
Our walls are all off-white, but hers
are painted sunset colors—rose
and apricot and yellow gold.

Her furniture is kind of plain.
But there are pillows and cushions
with sunflowers and watering cans,
roosters, geese, and cows.
They turn everything pretty.

> *Make yourselves at home, boys.*
> *I have to put the enchiladas*
> *in the oven to heat them up.*

"My pants are kind of dirty.
I don't want to mess up your couch."

> *Oh. Don't worry about that.*
> *Sylvester doesn't.*

"Who's Sylvester?"

Lily Points

Toward the sliding glass
door past the dining room
table. Standing just outside
on the shady back porch
is a big cocoa-colored dog.
It looks sort of like a huge
poodle, except fuzzier.

"What kind is he?"

A Labradoodle. Is it okay
if I let him in? He's friendly.

I would've guessed that
by his goofy dog grin. "Sure!"

I love dogs, and always wanted
one, but Mom and Dad both
said they were too much work.

Sylvester boings across the floor,
skids to a stop right in front of me.
"Hey, Sylvester." I reach out my hand
and he ducks his head under it,
asking to be petted. Hey, no problem.

You two get acquainted,
says Dad. *I'll see if Lily*
needs help in the kitchen.

"One second, Dad."

He looks anxious to join
Lily. Probably wants a kiss.

But he pauses long enough
to ask, *What is it?*

"Did you give Will some money?"

I did. Why do you ask?

"And Lily did, too?"

Yeah. I was a little short.

"What did he want it for?"

*He said his car needed an oil
change. You've got to keep up
on those things, you know.
Allowance money can't cover it.*

Sounds reasonable.
Why do I doubt it?

*It was nice he came to your game
and got to meet Lily, though, huh?*

Pretty sure he just came
to get the money, but all
I say is "Uh-huh. Real nice."

Should I Confess

That I'm scared for Will?
I'm not even sure exactly why,
so probably not. At least,
not until I have a solid reason.

I suspect . . .
I guess . . .
I think . . .
I worry . . .

Those are not solid reasons.

Dad goes to help Lily,
and Sylvester finds a ball,
drops it on the floor at my feet,
focuses his big brown eyes on me.

I understand what that means
more than I understand
what's going on with my brother.

"You wanna play fetch?"

It's like I flipped a switch.
He gets all excited, starts
wagging his tail, gives a little *yip*.

I think I've made a new friend.

"Can I take Sylvester outside
to play with the ball?" I yell.

Of course, agrees Lily.

Sylvester is already at the door.
He turns, telling me, *Hurry up!*
Check it out. I speak Labradoodle.

Lily has a huge fenced yard,
with grass and lots of flowers.
Guess Sylvester isn't much
into digging stuff up, because
it's all really pretty.

I stand on the porch, throw
the ball across the yard.
The dog is quick. Prefers
catching midair to chasing
on the ground. But either
way, he loves to play.

After twenty or thirty rounds,
he drops the ball by the door,
lies down beside it. Guess
we're officially finished.

"Good boy," I tell him.

His tail moves side to side,
slower than before. He's tired.
Come to think of it, so am I.
Tired and hungry.
Enchiladas, here I come!

Lily's a Super Cook

The enchiladas are as good
as any I've had in a restaurant.

By the time Dad and I are ready
to leave, I'm stuffed to the max.

Lily sends the leftovers home
for Will, or for us to snack on later.

Sylvester follows us to the door.
"See ya, boy. Next time we'll play longer."

Which means I figure we'll be back.
Dad definitely thinks so, too.

> *You don't always have to do
> the cooking,* he says to Lily.

> *We can certainly fire up the grill.
> I'm a decent barbecuer, eh, Trace?*

"Uh, sure, Dad. Maybe let Lily
help you out, though."

They both laugh, so they get
my not really so funny joke.

When Dad kisses Lily goodbye,
it only jabs a little.

Not as bad as last time.

Sunday Morning, I Sleep In

As the light grows brighter,
part of my brain insists
I need to open my eyes.

Another part is holding me
stuck in a really nice dream.
Will and I are playing keep-away
catch with Sylvester while Dad
barbecues and Mom sits on
a porch swing and sings.

It's a mash-up, but a happy one,
so when I finally wake up
all the way, I'm in a good mood.
Only I wish Mom and Sylvester
were really here.

My stomach growls, telling me
it's past time for breakfast,
so I get dressed. On my way
to the kitchen, I pass Will,
hunched over on the couch,
checking out my baseball glove,
which I must've left on the end table.

  He looks up with droopy eyes
  when I go by. *Hey. What's this?*

"The autograph? It's Victor
Sánchez's. He signed it yesterday."

I Give Him the Details

He actually seems impressed.

> *Wow. That's awesome.*
> *Victor Sánchez is a legend.*

"You could've met him, too.
Why did you leave so fast?"

> *Yeah, sorry. I had to meet*
> *up with someone.*

"I thought you were getting
your oil changed."

There it is—the throb
of blood in his temples.

It's not as funny as it was
when I was a little kid, though.

> *I had to do both. Oh, hey, dude.*
> *Who won your game, anyway?*

Way to change the subject.
"We did. Five–four. Like you care."

> Now the tips of his ears
> turn red. *I said I was sorry.*

"Yeah, Will, I know.
You're always sorry."

What difference does it make?
I turn my back on him.

Stomp into the kitchen, fling
open the fridge door.

I didn't even notice Dad,
reading a newspaper at the table.

His voice makes me jump.
Something wrong, Trace?

I could tell him. Should tell
him. But he looks relaxed.

And his eyes tell me he's happy.
Why ruin his mood? Why spoil the day?

"Oh, no. Everything's cool.
Didn't mean to jerk it so hard."

*Oh, good. There's a Dodgers game
on at one. Wanna watch?*

We used to watch them together
on his days off all the time.

But lately, he's been too busy.
"No Lily today or what, Dad?"

*No. She's chaperoning an event.
But she might stop by later.*

Guess I'm Good With That

Not that it matters.
But honestly, I like seeing
Dad with a smile most of the time.

Plus, there are perks. "Can I have
leftover enchiladas for breakfast?"

If there are any left, go for it.

There are, and I do.
It's the last day of spring break,
and it's nice to spend it with Dad.

Before the game starts,
we play some catch, just like
we used to do when I was little.
Mr. Cobb hears us out in the yard
and sticks his head over the fence.

Did I ever tell you about the time
I had a beer with Sandy Koufax?

Koufax pitched for the Dodgers
back before my dad was born.
He's a Major League Hall of Famer
and, according to Mr. Cobb,
a straight-up nice guy.

Did I ever tell you about touring
a brewery, and oo-ee, did that
place stink to high heaven!

Mr. Cobb talks so long
we miss the start of the game,
but Dad is too polite to say so.

He might talk even longer
except a car out front starts up
and we all look to see who it is.

Oh, there goes your Will, says
Mr. Cobb. *That boy sure does
come and go all hours. Does he
drive for that Uber or something?*

Nah, answers Dad. *He isn't old
enough. But you know teenagers.
They always have spring break plans.*

Like what kind, Dad?

At least it gives us a chance
to excuse ourselves, go inside.
It's the third inning by the time
we turn on the TV. No score,
so guess we didn't miss much.

But as the Dodgers come to bat,
I'm wondering why Mr. Cobb
seems to have noticed Will's
unusual schedule.

And why Dad mostly overlooks it.

It's Good

To go back to school,
where things make sense.

       A Days: science
              math
              computers
       B Days: social studies
              English
              PE
       C Days: library
              music
              art

I know what to expect,
what time to expect it.
The only variables I worry
about are the algebra kind.

Will drives us to Rainbow Charter
the same way he always does.
We listen to his favorite radio station,
which is mostly rap and hip-hop.
He knows all the words.
But today he doesn't sing along.

"How come you're so quiet?"

       Will shrugs. *Don't feel so good.*
       Think I ate something that
       didn't agree with my gut.

"You know what Dad always says."

He tries to smile. *Yeah. Nothing*
a decent poop couldn't cure.

Not so easy to do at school,
but maybe he should try.

He turns into the parking lot,
pulls into his assigned space.
But when I open my door,
he just sits, staring out the window.

"Aren't you coming inside?"

In a few. Probably. Trying to
decide if I should go home
instead. You head on in.

Suddenly, he jerks the driver's
door open, jams his head outside,
upchucks all over the pavement.

"Do you want me to call Dad?"

No. I feel a little better now.
But I'm going to take off.

"What about after school?"

Don't worry. I'll get you home.

Don't Worry

Seems like that's all I do
lately, at least when it comes
to my brother.

I stop by the office
before heading to class,
tell Mrs. Pearson, the school
secretary, that Will got sick.
I don't mention the puke
in the parking lot.

Too embarrassing.
Even if it wasn't me
who did it.

It's an A Day,
which means science
first block for my squad.
The students here are organized
into teams or squads, and we stay
together with our teammates
through all our core classes.

All the kids on my squad
are GATE, which means
our classwork is more difficult.

Must keep those ultra-curious
minds engaged is how Ms. Pérez
puts it. She's our science teacher.

As I half expected, we have
a new kid on our squad.

Hey, Trace, says Cat when
I come through the door.

You two know each other?
asks Ms. Pérez.

"Yeah. From Little League.
We're on the same team there, too."

*Good. Why don't the two of you
work together on today's lab?*

This quarter's STEM project:
design and build a workable robot.

We'll have lots of helpful videos
and a kit with basic parts,
but we can make it look however
we want and assign it a unique task.

Our math and computer science
classes will also be involved,
and at the end, there will be a challenge.

Epic!

Okay, It Does Mean

I'll be partnered with a girl
for all my A Day classes.
At this point, I'm guessing
that's not a bad thing.

Most girls are annoying.
A few in my class are kind of cute,
I guess, but the way they flock
together, always chirping
and cawing, reminds me of birds.

I doubt Cat is a chirper.
As we watch an introduction
to engineering video, she takes
notes. Sometimes she writes
down questions to ask Ms. Pérez.
I should probably be doing that, too.
"Hey. Can I copy your notes later?"

Cat shrugs. *They're for both
of us. It's called teamwork.*

After science, we break for lunch.
We don't have to stay with
our squads to eat or at recess.
I usually hang out with Bram.

Mostly because we're buddies,
but also because his MPU
(Mom Parental Unit) likes to bake
and sends pretty good treats.

I've never invited a girl
to join us. But here's the thing.
Cat doesn't know anyone here.
At least, I don't think so.

"Hey, Cat. You don't have to
have lunch with me if you'd rather . . ."

What? Go chirp with a flock of girls?

"Never mind. If you want,
come eat with Bram and me,
that is, if you brought your lunch."

     I did. Thanks, Trace.

We take our lunch boxes
outside, wait for Bram
on the grass beneath a big tree.
I squint, scoping out the parking lot.

     What are you looking at?

"Just trying to see if my brother's
car is out there. It's not. He got
sick right as we got here."

     Does he bring you every day?

"He's supposed to, but lately
he hasn't been too reliable."

Bram Comes out the Door

I wave him over.
He smiles until he notices
who's going to eat with us.

Hey, Bram, says Cat.

What are you doing here?

I go here now. Duh.

That's right. He wasn't there
when we talked about it
after the game on Saturday.
"She's on my squad.
We're doing this really cool—"

Why don't you eat with the girls?

*Mostly because I don't know
any of them. But I'll eat
by myself if you want me to.*

I think he's going to say
yeah, which would be bad,
because I don't want her to.
"No. Hang with us.
It's okay, right, Bram?"

He gives in. *Yeah. I guess.*

We unpack our lunches.

Cat and Bram inspect theirs,
but I know what's in mine
because I made it:

PB & J, which I have way too often.
One banana.
One juice pouch.
One granola bar.

"Is that all you're having?"
I ask Cat. "An avocado, crackers,
and a bunch of raw veggies?"

>   *Yeah*, comments Bram.
>   *You on a diet or something?*

>   *Hey, there's ranch dip*, she says.
>   *Anyway, I have a huge breakfast.*
>   *Which, in case you don't know,*
>   *should be your biggest meal*
>   *of the day. So, I like a light lunch.*

That might be, but when Bram
gives me the extra brownie
his mom made and I offer to split
it with her, Cat is happy to take it.

>   *Like, who turns down brownies?*

She's Steady

Like, she rolls with everything
tossed her way. So I ask,
"Hey, Cat. Why'd you guys
move to Vegas? I mean, why not
New York or Chicago or Paris?"

Dad got a coaching job at UNLV.

"Baseball, right? But their season
is most of the way over. Why now?"

They lost a coach not too long
ago. He died in a car wreck.

Oh, yeah. I heard about
that, says Bram.

He was my dad's friend.
They went to college together.
In fact, he got Dad the job.
It was supposed to start next year.

"Isn't it hard to change schools
now? Did you like your old one?"

It was okay. But I've changed
schools lots of times before,
so it's no big deal. It was harder
for my brother. He had to leave
this girl he really liked behind.

I thought you had two brothers.

Yeah, but only one of them moved
with us. Nicolás is a freshman.

"Does he go here, too?"

No. He's finishing the year online.
I could've done that, too, but
they don't offer advanced classes
for sixth graders. I'd be totally bored.

What about your other brother?

Cat frowns and she gets
this weird look in her eyes.

We don't know where Mateo is.
One day we woke up and he was gone.

"Like, kidnapped?"

That was one theory. But there
wasn't any ransom demand.
The cops think he ran away.

The Bell Rings

And that's probably good.
I want more info
about Cat's brother
but don't think I should ask.

Still, all through math
and computer science,
my mind wanders away
from what it should
stay focused on.

The more I get to know
Cat, the more it seems like
we have lots in common.

Baseball
GATE
Robot building
Messed-up brothers

Weird how two
way different people,
from way different kinds
of families, can share
things like that.

Wonder if Victor Sánchez
is going out with a lady
who can cook
awesome enchiladas.

After School

There's a line of cars
out front, waiting.
One by one, kids climb
into the appropriate vehicle.

Bram's MPU is near the front,
so he's gone right away.
I don't see Will.
Wonder if I'll have to
call Dad about a ride.

Cat waits with me.
I recognize her car
as it approaches,
but Victor isn't driving.
It's the lady I saw that first
day Cat came to practice.

"Is that your mom?"

>   No. Iva is Dad's personal assistant.

"And chauffeur?"

>   Only when he's busy.

"Does she make enchiladas?"

>   I don't know. Why?

"No reason. See you tomorrow."

I'm the Last Kid

Left standing here,
and I'm just about to go
back inside to dig out
my phone when I see
Will's car come zooming
along the boulevard.

He whips it
into the entrance,
screeches to a stop
in front of me, drops
the passenger window.

Get in, dude. Let's go!

I duck to look past
the opened glass.

"Guess you're feeling better?"

Yeah, man. Come on!

He's all fired up, fingers tapping
the steering wheel, like he's
had too much coffee or something.
I kind of want to walk home.
But it's three miles from here,
and that would be one very hot stroll.

When I get in the car,
he takes off without waiting

for me to strap in, turns
the opposite direction from home.

"Where are we going?"

> The mall. I need new shoes,
> and Foot Locker's having a sale.

I glance down at his feet.
Those Adidas look okay.
Better than mine, in fact.
But whatever. I like the mall,
especially on weekdays
when it isn't so crowded.

It's a pretty good sale.
Will picks up a $200 pair
of Nikes for $129. But now
I'm wondering where
the money came from.

"Hey. You still have to pay
me back, you know."

> Oh, yeah, right.

He hands me a twenty.

> Don't worry. I'll get you
> the rest, and I'll spring
> for the food court now, too.

We Head That Direction

But on the way over, Will spots
someone clear across the mall.
His eyes narrow, like he's looking
real hard to make sure the guy
is who he thinks he is.

> *Hey. I need to talk to my buddy*
> *over there. I'll meet you at*
> *Hot Dog on a Stick, okay?*

"Okay." If it's corn dogs
for dinner, I'm having two.
Plus, the lemonade is good.

I take my time,
glancing back over
my shoulder, playing
private investigator.
What's Will up to?

I see him reach into
his pocket for . . .
money? He keeps it
tucked into his fist, and—

> *Trace?*

My head snaps to the left.
"Skye. Wow. I haven't
seen you in a long time."

It has been a while.
How are you? And how's Will?

I shrug. "Up and down.
Some days are better
than others. He's right
over there." I point.

Skye
       follows my finger.
Smiles
       when she sees him.
Scowls
       when she notices who he's with.

"What's the matter?"

       Nothing. It's just that guy
       he's talking to goes to my school.
       He creeps me out.

"Why?"

       I don't know. He's just off.
       Some people say he sells drugs.

I think of the money
balled up in Will's hand.
But when I look over,
they're just goofing around.

Still, There's Something

About the other dude that is . . .
Yeah, "creepy" works.

He's tall, but his bony
legs poke out of his shorts
like drumsticks, and
his peach-colored shirt
is probably three sizes too big.

His hair is way long, thin,
and even from here I can see
it could use shampoo.
Plus, his skin looks bleached,
like the sun never touches it.

He reminds me of a corpse,
or maybe a vampire.

> *Well, better run. I'm supposed*
> *to meet a friend in a few.*
> *Tell Will I still miss him.*

"Do you think he's okay?
I mean, hanging out with him?"
I tilt my head toward the two of them.

> *I don't think Will's been okay*
> *for quite a while, you know?*

I wish she wasn't right.

I Wait for Will

For a long time, sitting here
breathing in the yummy scent
of fried sausages on sticks.

My stomach growls,
and I decide to spend some
of the twenty he gave me,
even though he still owes
me forty more, and promised
this food was on him.

One hot dog on a stick.
One cheese—pepper jack—on a stick.
One order of fries.
One lemonade.

That's *most* of the twenty.
And way too much tasty grease.

I'm munching away
when Will finally appears.

> *Guess you were hungry.*

"Guess I sat here long
enough to figure maybe
I'd better eat or starve to death.
This cost me sixteen bucks, BTW."

> *I'll get it back to you. I barely
> have enough to cover my food.*

I Shove a French Fry

In my mouth to keep from
saying something mean
or asking a question
he won't answer anyway.

He manages to pay
for three corn dogs plus
a drink, joins me at the table.

I swallow the bite in my mouth.
"I saw Skye. She said to tell
you she still misses you."

It's enough to make him mad,
don't ask me why. I can tell
by the way he goes all stiff.

But all he says is, *Cool.*

I take another bite.
Chew slowly, deciding
if I should spit it out.
Not the food, the question
that's bugging me.

He's going to get mad.
But I don't care.
"People at her school
think your vampire friend
sells drugs. Does he?"

Now Will goes ballistic.

> *She told you that? Well, you*
> *listen to me. As far as I know,*
> *he does not sell drugs. Are you*
> *saying you think I buy them?*

People turn to stare,
so I try to calm him down.

"No, no. That's not what I meant.
It's just, the dude creeps Skye
out, and me, too. He looks like
Vladimir Tod, right?"

> *Vlad—Who's that?*

"You know, the vampire.
From that book *Eighth Grade*
Bites. Well, it's actually a series—"

> *I don't know what you're talking*
> *about. Finish eating, okay?*

At least he quit yelling.

We Toss Our Trash

And start toward the exit
closest to where Will parked.

Ahead, between us and the door,
there's some kind of commotion.
Two people are arguing,
but I can only see one, who's tall
and standing in front of the other,
back turned toward us.

Security is nowhere in sight.
A young couple passes the trouble
and I think the guy says something,
but then he steers his girl quickly away.

As we get closer, I recognize
the drumstick legs and baggy
shirt. The tall one is the vampire,
harassing someone smaller.

He turns slightly and his victim
comes into view. It's a slender
girl with brass-blond hair, and
I'm pretty sure I know her.

Her voice is also familiar.
Do not touch me again!

"Hey," I tell Will. "That's Skye."
She's trying to move past
Vlad, who steps in her way.

Come on, baby, he sneers.
I'm not going to hurt you.

He reaches out, grabs
her arm with one hand,
runs the other hand down
the length of her cheek.

Leave me alone! Skye sounds
totally freaked out.

"Do something, Will."

Like what?

"He's *your* 'friend.'
Tell him to stop."

Skye can take care of herself.

He can't be serious!
Fine. I'll handle it.

I run.
Insert myself between them.
Nudge Skye backward.
Look into the dude's eyes.
They're a long way up.

"Quit bothering her."

He Looks Down

And what I see in his red-
rimmed eyes makes me shiver.
No fear. No apology.

More like amusement,
but it's the kind he might
feel for a pesky fly while
holding one of those bug-
zapper things.

He reaches around me,
pets Skye's hair.

> *Whatcha gonna do if I won't,*
> *little man? Beat me up?*

Where's Will?
I puff up as big as I can.
"I could try."

> *No, Trace,* says Skye. *It's okay.*
> *We can just leave. Right, Jackson?*

Finally, Will interferes.
He taps Jackson (dumb name
for a vampire) on the shoulder.

> *That's my little brother.*
> *He's just a kid. You don't want*
> *to hurt him, do you?*

Fists Raised

Jackson wheels around,
ready to let fly.

Will backs away, ducks.

But when the vampire
sees who's standing there,
he drops his hands.

Nah. Don't want to hurt him.
In fact, I gotta respect the tadpole.
But you—he points at me—
oughta be more careful. Some
people aren't as nice as me.

"You're so nice you pick on
girls. Haven't you ever heard
of this thing called consent?"

Everyone freezes.
But, hey, I'm not about
to wait for him to change
his mind. "Come on, Skye."

I turn and push her toward
the exit. As we leave, I hear
Jackson laugh way too loud.

Your brother has more grit
than brains, he tells Will.

Actually, I'm shaking.
But I'm also proud of myself.
And disappointed in Will.

Skye and I wait for him
just outside the door.

>*Thanks, Trace. He followed
>me all around the mall.*

"That guy's a goon."

>*Exactly. A nasty goon.*

"What happened to the friend
you were supposed to meet?"

>*He's running a little late.*

"He?"

>*Kevin. My boyfriend.*

"Boyfriend? But what about
Will? You said you miss him."

>*I do. I still love him, and probably
>always will. You can't turn off love
>like the lights. But sometimes
>you have to move on.*

You Can't Turn Off Love

I hope that's true.

It kind of looks that way
when Will finally comes outside.
And it's awkward.

He exits the building,
tense and scowling.
But when he sees Skye,
everything softens:

>   his shoulders
>   his jaw
>   his eyes.

He stands there,
almost smiling,
staring at Skye,
who stands there,
staring right back.

Bet ol' Kevin wouldn't
like this one bit.

Finally, Skye opens her mouth.

>   *Good to see you, Will.*
>   *Thanks for coming to the rescue.*

Wait. What?
It wasn't exactly Will
who came to the rescue.

I could say something.
Will should say something.

He does. *No problem.*
But FYI, Jackson's bark
is worse than his bite.

It's one of Grandpa's sayings.
It means Jackson might be rude,
but he wouldn't actually hurt her.
I'm not sure that's true, though.

And neither is Skye.
Her face flares bright red.

He was all over me, Will.
I can't believe you're defending
him. Your little brother understood.

Trace doesn't know Jackson
like I do. He's a friend.

You used to have better friends.

That's for sure.

I have to go. Is it okay
if I give you a hug, Trace?

"Yeah. It's cool."
See, now, that's consent.

Will and I Don't Talk Much

On the ride home.
To break the silence,
he turns up the radio.

> Super loud.
> Drake booms
> out the open windows.

At every stop sign,
every red light,
people in other cars
look around, trying
to find the source
of the pounding bass.

I tune it out as best I can,
consider the last couple
of hours. What is going
on with my brother?

Like, why

> would he make me
> be the one forced
> into playing hero?

And why

> would he stick
> up for the vampire
> instead of Skye?

I Thought

He cared about her.
He used to.
I'm positive about that.

Did he turn off
love like flipping
a light switch?

He'll get mad
if I ask. But I'm getting
used to that.

So here goes, anyway.
"Hey, Will?"
Not sure he heard me.

I reach out, turn
down the radio.
"Do you still love Skye?"

What? Mean voice. *Why?*

"Just wondering."
No response.
"Well, do you?"

None of your business.

He didn't say no.
And that kind of
says everything.

Back to the Routine

Homework
Dinner (already accomplished)
Shower
TV or a video game
Bed

Day done.

Next morning:

Breakfast
Brush teeth
Off to school

Looks like Will's going to stay
today. When he parks, I remind
him, "I've got practice later."

He answers with a grunt.
That's the most he's said
to me since yesterday.

B Block today is ace
because in social studies
we're learning about ancient
Greece, and in ELA we get to
write our own myth.

*You have to set it in Greece,
though,* instructs Mr. Benton.
No Percy Jackson in New York City.

The Research Is Interesting

In ancient Greece,
more than 2,500 years ago,
they had city-states, which
kind of inspired the states
here in the good old USA.

A lot of people were slaves,
who had to work for free,
sort of like the African American
slaves in our country's past.

But there were also these
philosopher guys like Plato
and Socrates. They were
all into deep thought
when there was no internet
or even books to help them
figure out stuff, like how
the universe worked.

They studied the sky
and wanted to know
what it meant when the sun
or moon seemed to move.

Were they in motion?
Or were we?
Math. Science. Logic.
They trusted
in those things.

They probably didn't believe
in the gods and goddesses
most people worshipped
back then. According to
their mythology, each of
those gods was in charge
of different things, like war
or love, death or learning.

Twelve of them supposedly
lived in Zeus's palace, on
top of Mount Olympus,
the highest mountain in Greece.

Writing my myth makes me think.
If I lived a long, long time
ago, would I have believed
Zeus was an all-powerful god?

Or would I have stared at
Mount Olympus and decided
I should climb it, not to see
what was on top, but to get
an awesome look at
the real world below?

Last Class

At the end of the day is PE.
Today, and probably for the rest
of the year, that happens inside,
out of the hot Vegas sun.

We're moving to music.
Which, I guess, sounds better
than dancing, at least to the guys.
Some of them complain anyway,
but our teacher just laughs.

> *Professional football players*
> *do ballet to improve balance*
> *and flexibility. So it won't hurt*
> *you to rock 'n' roll a little.*

We're listening to Ms. Kendall's
personal playlist, which is a mix
of oldies and newer alternative rock.
Suddenly, a familiar voice is singing
her latest song. It's like she's right here.

Breathing hard from effort
and surprise, I stop moving.
Cat's right behind me.

> *What's wrong?*

"Nothing. Only, that's my mom."

Hearing Her Sing

Makes me feel proud.
Makes me feel sad.
Makes me feel happy.
Makes me feel lonely.

After class, we collect
our backpacks and, time
to go home, leave the building.

Cat walks outside with me.

> *I didn't know Serene Etienne*
> *was your mom. That's awesome.*

"You know who she is?"

> *Who doesn't?*

"She's not really that famous.
Obsidian is kind of a niche band."

> *Niche?*

"Yeah. Not so mainstream.
A smaller but loyal fan base
that loves everything they do."

> *My mom is one of those fans.*
> *She's even seen them play.*

It's the first time I've heard
her mention her mother.
Which makes me wonder.

"You said that lady who drove
you the other day was your dad's
personal assistant, right? Why
didn't your mom just drive you?"

She's still in LA.

"Are you parents divorced?"

No. But Mom didn't want to move
until we find out about my brother.
She keeps hoping he'll come home.

"That must be hard."

She nods. I miss them both.
But Mateo made everyone worry,
even before he disappeared.
He got into drugs. Joined a gang.
Sometimes I wish Mom would let him go.

I think I can relate.
Speaking of the devil.

"Here comes Will.
See you at practice."

Will Doesn't Wait

For me to follow him.
He jumps in his car,
backs out of his spot,
and for a second
I think he's planning
to leave without me.

But then he circles the lot,
pulls up at the curb,
motions for me to get in.

I'm still thinking about Cat
when we start toward home.

"Wanna hear something
cool? My friend Cat knows
Mom's music. She said
her mother loves Obsidian
and has seen them in concert."

> *Cat? You mean the new girl*
> *player on your team?*
> *Since when is she your friend?*

It's kind of a good question,
actually. We didn't know
each other at all a week ago.

"I guess since now."

I've Never Had a Friend

Like Cat before.
I mean, yeah, because
she's a girl.

I can't even call her a buddy.

I never thought about
having a girl for a friend.

Not really sure why except,
I guess, I never knew
they could play baseball
or design robots.

But even if she couldn't
do those things, I'd like Cat.
She's smart, funny, real.

Girls always seemed
kind of fake, with their
makeup, glitter, polished nails.

Maybe I should've looked
harder, deeper, longer.

Because Catalina Sánchez
can't be the only awesome
girl in the world.

Right?

Will Pulls Up

In front of the house.
I get out of the car.
He doesn't.
I motion: *Open the window.*
"Aren't you coming in?"

Nah. I've got somewhere to be.

"What about practice?"

Something wrong with your bike?

"No, but—"

Coolio. See you on the far side.

Coolio?
Where did that come from?

The thought
barely materializes
before he takes off.

Oh well.
Not exactly a surprise.

I let myself in,
change into my uniform,
grab my cleats, and put
them in my gym bag.

Now, where's my glove?

Not on my dresser.
Not in my closet.
Not on the chair.

Where did I leave it?
Oh, yeah.
In the living room.
But when I go to find
it, it's nowhere in sight.

I look in the sofa cushions.
Under the coffee and end tables.
Beneath Dad's La-Z-Boy.

Nope.
Nope.
Nope.

I look in the kitchen.
In the bathroom.
In the hall closet.

Nope.
Nope.
Nope.

The last time I saw it was . . .

Sunday

The morning after the game.
Will was holding it,
checking out the autograph.

I run back to his room.
Look under his bed.
Dig through his drawers.
Search his closet.

No sign of my glove.
It's disappeared.

Dad might yell at me
for leaving it out,
but he wouldn't hide it.

The last person to touch
it was Will. He must be
the one who took it.

But why?

He knows I need it to play.
Thanks to him, I don't have
enough money to replace it.
And even if I did, a new one
would have to be broken in,
and it wouldn't have . . .

Victor Sánchez's autograph.

No Wonder

He took off so fast.
I try calling him, but
of course he doesn't answer.

Just you wait, Will.
Just you wait.

And now I'm late for practice.
I decide to go anyway,
so my coaches don't think
I flaked out on them.

Even if I can't play our next
game because I don't have a glove.

Just you wait, Will.
Just you wait.

I jump on my bike.
Pedal it like a madman,
because I am one.
And not just mad, but furious.
It seems like I feel that way
more and more lately.

All because of my brother.

They say exercise is good
for releasing stress
and anger. I hope so.
Will should hope so, too.

Batting Practice

Is over.
Everyone is in the field.
Trevor is pitching.
He's, like, last string,
but everyone deserves
the chance to get better.

I lean my bike against the fence.
Approach Coach Hal,
who motions for me to wait.
So I sit, watching,
until he comes over.

What's up?

I tell him my glove
seems to have vanished.
That I looked all over
but just couldn't find it.

*I see. Well, you can't play
without one, can you?*

"No, but I didn't even know
it was gone until after school."

*Tell you what. Practice
with mine for what's left
of our time today. But have
one by Saturday. Deal?*

No-Brainer

Coach's glove is too big,
but I make it work
for the half hour remaining.

Afterward, Bram and Cat
tag-team me.

Bram: *What happened?*

Me: gives information.

Cat: *Are you sure it was Will?*

Me: huge eye roll.

Bram: *You got Victor Sánchez's
autograph? How? When?*

Me: gives information.
Bram stares at Cat.

Cat: *Not my fault he's my father.*

Bram: *Why didn't you tell me?*

Me: claims forgetfulness.
Bram stares at me.

"Sorry, man. I would've showed
you today. But now my glove
is gone, and so is the autograph."

Cat: *If it's useful, I can forge*
Dad's signature. I've done it
on permission slips.

Bram and I spit laughter.
Not just because she's funny,
but also because she's probably
not even kidding.

What? Comes in handy.

Bram changes the subject.
So, what are you going to do
about your glove?

"Guess I'll have to ask Dad
to buy me another one."

What about Will? Shouldn't
he be the one who buys it?

"If he got rid of my old one,
yeah, he should. But he won't."

Even if he did, it would be
with your money, observes Bram.

What do you mean? Cat asks.

"Long story."

But Bram Says

It's not really so long,
so I go ahead and tell it.

     Cat whistles. *That's bad.*
     I think your brother's in
     need of an intervention.

          What's that? asks Bram.

     It means getting involved
     to try to change things
     before it's too late.

"Too late to what?"

     Turn back around. Like Mateo.

"But your mom thinks
he can turn back around."

     She shrugs. *Maybe, maybe*
     not. If she really believes it,
     she's fooling herself, and I
     doubt she does. But she refuses
     to give up on him. Yet.

"Did you give up on him?"

     She looks away. *I had to.*
     I couldn't be sad every day.

Her Words Sink In

As I bike home.
                    Pedal

                              I

                    Pedal

                              couldn't

                    Pedal

                              be

                    Pedal

                              sad

                    Pedal

                              every

                    Pedal

                              day.

Cat gave up
on Mateo.
                    Pedal

                              I

                    Pedal

                              don't

                    Pedal

                              want

                    Pedal

                              to

                    Pedal

                              give

                    Pedal

                              up

                    Pedal

                              on

                    Pedal

                              Will.

He doesn't care.

        Pedal

                . . . your

        Pedal

                brother's

        Pedal

                in

        Pedal

                need

        Pedal

                of

        Pedal

                an

        Pedal

                intervention.

I don't want to
push too hard.

        Pedal

                If

        Pedal

                I

        Pedal

                do,

        Pedal

                what

        Pedal

                if

        Pedal

                he

        Pedal

                just

        Pedal

                disappears?

185

Home Again

Alone again,
I text Dad.

Hey, Dad?
I need a new glove
or I can't play Sat.

Now I shower, change
clothes, go find something
to microwave for dinner.

I'm halfway through
my chicken Alfredo
when I get a text
back from Dad.

Where's your old glove?

Don't know.
Looked all over
but couldn't find it.
Left it somewhere?

I thought about
that answer with hot
water streaming
through my shampooed
hair and down my back.

If I said Will took it,
he'd only deny it, and
everything would blow up.

Last time
that happened,
Will took off.
What if this time
he doesn't come back?
It would be my fault.

No, I have to figure
out how to fix
things myself.

>Then it's your responsibility
>to pay for a new one.

I was afraid
he'd say that.
A decent glove
is at least fifty dollars.

I don't have enough money.

>Where's your savings?

Oh, man. Now what?
Quick. Think fast!

I loaned most of it to Bram.

>He'd better pay you back.
>And I hope you've learned
>a lesson. Darn shame, too.
>The autograph and all.

Sure, Rub It In

So, what now?

I can tell Will
he'd better pay me back
or else I'll tell Dad he took
my money and my glove.

But if the reason he took
it is that he needed
even more money,
I'm sure it's gone already.

I can talk to Mr. Cobb
about doing some chores.
But he lives on a "fixed
income," which means
he doesn't have much money
and can only pay me
three bucks an hour.

There won't be time to save
up enough before Saturday.

Still, I wash my fork
and glass, toss
the microwavable container
in the trash, go next door.
Mr. Cobb is sitting on
his front porch, staring
at the darkening sky.

"Hey, Mr. C. What's up?"

Not much at the moment.
Sit down for a spell.
What can I do for you?

"I was hoping maybe
you had some work for me . . ."
I tell him what I need
without mentioning Will.

Hmm. As a rule, baseball gloves
don't walk off on their own.

"Yeah. It's kind of weird."

I wish I could lend you the money
and let you work it off, but
my retirement check doesn't
get here until the first of the month.

"That's okay. I still need
to save up for a new one."

You come on over after school
tomorrow. Weeds are not
in short supply around here.
Oh, and the ivy needs attention.

Ugh. That's one of the worst
jobs. Lots of bugs in the ivy.
But if it needs to be done, I'll do it.

I Should Go Do My Homework

But it's kind of nice
having someone to talk to.
It gets lonely at home.
"Hey, Mr. Cobb. Do you
have a brother?"

   No. A sister. Why?

"Did you ever have to
worry about her?"

   He laughs kind of quietly.
   *Not really. I think she had
   to worry about me, though.*

"How come?"

   *I was a . . . I guess you could
   call me a troublemaker.*

"Really?"

   He nods. *A regular rebel.
   As far as I was concerned,
   rules did not apply to me.
   Ended up I had a choice:
   go to jail or join the army.*

   *I figured Vietnam was better
   than lockup, but it was
   its own kind of prison.*

"You were in that war?"
I've heard of it but don't
know much about it.
"What was it like?"

He goes back to staring
at the sky, which is now
decorated with stars.

The air was suffocating—hot,
wet, and it carried the smell
of jungle and sweat and rot.
They told us fear was our friend,
which would've been good
if I needed a buddy. I didn't.

I was nineteen, and figured
every day would be my last.
I sure didn't want to die,
but death was always close by.

The hair on the back
of my neck prickles.

You want to know the most
ironic thing about that?
The military in general, and
war in particular, are all about
rules. I learned to respect them.

All I can say is "Wow."

I Start to Get Up

But Mr. Cobb stops me.

> *Hold on a minute.*
> *You're worried about*
> *your brother, aren't you?*

What is he, psychic?
But I have no reason
not to say, "Yeah."

> *Do you think he had*
> *something to do with*
> *your glove disappearing?*

It's embarrassing,
but, "Probably."

> *Have you told your dad?*

Even more
embarrassing. "No."

> *Why not?*

"I don't . . ." But I do know.

"It's just, when Dad gets mad
at Will, they fight, and . . .
I don't want them to get hurt."

He's quiet for a minute,
like he's trying to find
the right words.

>*I see. You're a good boy,*
>*Trace. You love your brother*
>*and want to protect him.*

>*But here's the deal, and I*
>*hope you'll think about it.*

>*Looking back, I wish*
>*I would've talked to my parents*
>*about the stuff I was struggling*
>*with. Things might have gone*
>*a whole lot differently.*

Parents.
Hang on.
I have two.

"Okay. I get it. Thanks,
Mr. Cobb . . ."

Wait.

"You won't say anything
to Dad, right?"

>*Not if you don't want me to.*
>*But you really should.*

Will's Home

When I get back.
I can hear him clunking
around in the kitchen,
fixing something to eat.

I march right up to him,
stick my face three inches
away from his.

"Where's my glove?"

What glove?

"Don't even! Why did
you take it? I can't play
without a glove, Will."

Why do you think I took it?

"Because the last time
I saw it, you were holding it."

Anger flashes in his eyes.
Is that what you told Dad?

"No. I covered for you,
don't ask me why. I told
him I left it somewhere."

Okay. Good. I don't need
trouble with Dad.

"What about trouble with me?
I need a glove before Saturday.
What happened to mine?"

Will puts a take-and-bake
pizza in the oven.

I'm supposed to stick to
the microwave, but Dad
says Will's mature enough
to bake stuff without
burning down the house.

I kind of doubt it.

                    Finally, he says, *Okay, look.*
                    I took it to show a friend.

A gasp of hope.
"So, it's in your car?"

                    Well, no. I forgot to lock
                    my car and someone took it.

"You mean, stole it."

                    Yeah. That's where I went
                    after school today. To try
                    and get it back. I thought
                    I knew who had it, but no.

His Story

Makes sense.
Sort of.
I think it's a lie.
But even if it's not,
he still took my glove
and now I don't have one.

"You already owed me
money. Now you owe
me a glove, too. Dad says
it's my responsibility,
but the truth is, it's yours."

*I know. I'm sorry. I'll make
things right as soon as I can,
but right now, I'm broke.*

How is that possible?

The buzzer goes off,
and Will pulls his pizza
out of the oven, takes it
over to the table.

Want some?

"Nah. I already ate."

He digs in, slurping the sauce
and making a bunch of other
gross eating sounds.

"You're disgusting."

Yeah, but everything tastes
better when some of it
leaks out of your mouth.

That makes no sense.
Nothing he does makes
sense anymore. But as I study
him, something strikes me.

His face hasn't twitched
once since I got all up in it.

Come to think of it,
it's been a while since
I've noticed the tic
that used to be so obvious.

Also, though I saw a quick
flash of rage earlier, lately
he hasn't seemed so mad
at the universe all the time.

"I'm going to do my homework."

Good plan. I mean,
one of us should.

I'm Working

On my Greek myth
when my phone buzzes.
It's a number I don't recognize,
but I pick up anyway.

Will taught me how to prank
sales calls, which I only
get once in a while,
by pretending I'm old
and senile, or a serial killer.
Or both.

I'm kind of looking forward
to that, so I answer in
a crotchety voice,
"Who's there? Is that
you, Martha?"

There's a long silence
on the other end.

      But then, *Trace?*

It's a girl. That's new. "Cat?"

      Yeah.

Weird. "How did you
get my number?"

      From Bram. Duh.

Bram. Right. Double
duh. "What's going on?"

> I was wondering what your dad
> said about your glove.

"He said it was up to me
to replace it. I can't by Saturday."

> I was afraid of that. Did you
> ask your brother about it?

"Yeah. He said someone
stole it out of his car."

She pauses, then mumbles
something to someone not me.

> Nicolás says you should check
> out the pawnshops.

"Good idea. They'd probably
want me to buy it back, though.
Which still doesn't help much."

> We'll figure something out.
> See you tomorrow.

Pawnshops

Are places you go when
you need money fast.
Vegas is crawling with them,
mostly because of the casinos.

Dad says gambling can be fun
for some people, but for others
it's an addiction. Even after
losing a whole lot of money,
they believe just one more bet
will win it all back and then
they'll get rich. Dad also says
they didn't build those giant
casinos by giving money away.

Anyway, if people need cash
fast, they take valuables
like jewelry or electronics
into a pawnshop, which gives
them a small fraction of what
those things are worth.
Then the pawnshop sells
them for a lot more.

Now, a used baseball glove
wouldn't be worth a lot all
on its own, but it would be with
a Victor Sánchez autograph.

So Much for My Myth

My brain has wandered
out of Greece, off the page,
and on to other things.

Will.
Gloves.
Pawnshops.
Casinos.
Dad.
Lily.
Mom.

The last hits me like a fist.
It's only been, like, a couple
of weeks since we talked,
but why hasn't she called
to check up on Will?

Called.

That works two ways.
Why haven't I called her?

I look at the clock.
8:16 p.m. Pacific.
I have no idea what time
zone she's in, or what
she's up to right now.

I wouldn't want to bother . . .

Hold On

If a call from me
bothers her,
that's her problem,
not mine.

I could text her.
But I want her to hear
my voice on the message
I'm asked to leave.

"Hey, Mom.
It's Trace.
We haven't talked
since I called you
about Will.

"I thought maybe
you'd care enough
to see how he's doing.
Not good, by the way.

"If it's late where
you are, I'm sorry.
I don't want to bug you,
but I just need to know.

"Are you there?
Are you okay?
Are you alive?"

I Don't Expect

Her to call me back tonight.
But she does.
Was it my last question?

> Hello, Trace. I'm so sorry
> it's been radio silence.

Hearing her voice
makes me happy
makes me sad
makes me mad
makes me lonely.

> It's just, between gigs
> and travel, I've been—

"Super busy. I know."

> Yeah. I think about you
> and Will all the time, though.

"Sure, Mom."

> Seriously. How's everyone?

"Dad has a girlfriend."
Whoa. Slipped right on out.

> Oh. That's wonderful.
> I mean, you like her, right?

"Sure. Lily's cool. It's just . . ."

What?

"She's not you. I miss you."

Oh, Trace. I miss you, too.
But I think it's good your dad
has found someone special.
Nobody wants to be alone. I—

"He's not alone! He has me."

It's not the same thing.
You'll understand one day.

She asks about school.
I tell her about robots.

She asks about Little League.
I tell her about Cat and her dad.

She asks about summer plans,
if we have any that might
interfere with a Colorado visit.

"I don't think so. Why?
Does this mean one might
happen?" I shake off a flutter
of excitement. Even if she says
yes, it won't be a promise.

I do hope so. The band's finalizing
the summer tour schedule now,
so I'll try to fit it in once we're set.

Not even a yes.

Finally, she asks, Okay, so
what about Will? What now?

I tell her about my glove.
She says it was a mistake.

I tell her about my money.
She says he'll pay me back.

I tell her Will thinks he'll die young.
She says all kids think that.

I tell her I wish she'd come see
for herself what's going on.

Oh, Trace. I'm just—

"Are you still in Colorado?"

No. We're at Tahoe now. It's nice.
The club where we're playing
is right on the beach. Off-season,
so it's not too crowded.

Lake Tahoe

Is maybe five hundred miles
from here. Far, but not nearly
as far as clear across the country.

"You're so close! When your
gig is up, can you come?"

> *Maybe. We're here for eight*
> *weeks. And there's stuff coming*
> *up after. But I will if I can.*

"School will be out by then.
It will be hot, but we could go
mountain biking in the actual
mountains. Or go to the lake, or—"

> *Easy now. Your dad might*
> *have other plans. But I promise*
> *we'll talk about it, okay?*

Talk about it sounds like
not gonna happen. But the idea
of seeing her twice in one
summer makes me so happy!
"Please, Mom. We need you."

> *That quiets her for a minute.*
> *I'll do my best. I've got to run.*

"Okay, Mom. Good
night . . . Wait!"

Wait

There's one more
thing I have to say.
Why haven't I
said it already?

"I love you."

One more thing
I need to hear.
Why hasn't she
said it already?

Love you, too.
Always and forever.

I really hope
she means it.

Give my love to Will.

"Okay."

By the time
the second syllable
clears my lips,
she's deserted me.

Again.

Suddenly, I Need to Play

The keyboard is in the living room.
Luckily, Will isn't watching TV.

I sit.
Power up.
My hands settle
on the keys.

Usually I'd play
something with a driving
beat, but tonight a beautiful
classical piece calls to me.

I open my music book,
turn to Debussy's
"Clair de lune."

Most kids would probably
only know this song
because it was in *Ocean's Eleven*.

But it's also one of Mom's
favorites. That's not the only
reason it reminds me of her.

The name means "Moonlight,"
and the soft chords and gentle
melody are like waves
of light beneath my hands.

It's beautiful.

Like my mom.

And I barely have
to look at the music.

It's like my fingers
understand exactly
how it should sound
by remembering her face.

Surfing moonlight.

Halfway

Through the piece,
Will wanders in from
the kitchen.

Why are you playing that?

I don't stop.
"Because I like it.
It makes me feel good."

It's slow. Why do you like it?

I have no reason
not to say, "Because
it reminds me of Mom."

Mom! Who's that?

His voice is kind of slurred.
Still, "You know who she is."

I forgot. Remind me?
Not like she ever does.

"I just talked to her,
Will. She said to tell
you she loves you."

You talked to her? Guessing
you must've called her.

Okay, So He's Right

And he knows it.
I don't have to admit it.
But I do feel the need
to defend our mom.

"She's doing the best
she can. She's just
really, really busy."

>   *Heard it before, thanks.*
>   *Dozens of times.*

"Well, I'm not giving
up on her yet."

>   *Why would you?*
>   *She didn't leave because of you.*
>   *She left because of me.*

I've thought the same
thing myself. And yet,
I say, "No she didn't.
She left because of her music."

>   *Okay, Trace. Whatever.*
>   *You keep playing boring*
>   *songs and dreaming*
>   *about Mom coming home.*
>   *I'm going to take a shower.*

Boom. See ya.

My Head

Feels like someone's playing
Ping-Pong inside it, thoughts
bouncing this way and that,
side to side, against my skull.

I start to play another song
Mom taught me a long time
ago. It's called "The Sound
of Silence." When I jump in,
it's the original, kind of soft
version by this group
named Simon & Garfunkel.

But I start to pick up speed,
and play with more volume
and power, more like Will's
favorite version of this song
by a band called Disturbed.

And it's still the same song—
Mom's version, and Will's—
and that seems so right,
it quiets the ping-ponging
in my brain, sharpens the focus.

I drop back down from forte
(loud) to piano (soft).
I love music.
Mom gave it to me.
I hate music.
It took her away.

I'm Mostly Amused

By it in C Day music class
this morning. We're playing
recorders, and not everyone
is exactly talented at it.

Just doing a simple scale
is too much for a couple.
Bram happens to be one.

"Dude. What was that?"

He laughs. *The key of X-Y-Z?*

"Even if they went past G,
each key is only one letter."

Tell that to my recorder.

*Okay, class. Let's try that
again, says Mrs. Marone.
Once you've conquered it,
we'll move on to Mozart.*

She's joking. By the time
class ends, we've managed
a bad "Three Blind Mice."

Some music is more like poison.

On My Way to Lunch

I notice Cat talking
to a knot of girls.

Woo-boy.

I'm glad she's trying
to make friends, but
Leah and Sara and Star
are, like, the most "popular"
girls in our class.

That equals the most
stuck-up, and the "in crowd"
doesn't accept new
members easily.

Still, Leah caws a laugh,
so loud it's obvious
she wants people to hear.

The others smile, but
it's the fake kind of smile
that means they're just
going along with Leah.

Now Cat says something
else, and if evil glares
could drop someone
in their tracks, she'd be
flat on the ground.

But it's her turn to laugh.

Cat Sees Me

And waves, then follows
me outside.
Bram's already
staked out a place,
so we sit with him.

"You joining the Mean
Girls Club?" I ask Cat.

Nah. Just messing with them.

Like, how? asks Bram.

I asked if they like sports.
Leah said sure, as long
as the players are cute.
Star and Sara were all like,
yeah. If the players are cute.

So then I asked if they thought
I was cute. I guess they didn't
think that was very funny.

No way! But Bram
sounds impressed.

That is so Cat.

And now she does something
unexpected, and yet still so Cat.

She Digs

Through her backpack,
and I figure she's looking
for her lunch.

But that's not what comes
out of there.

What does is a well-worn
baseball glove. She offers
it to me, and I see it's signed.

Yes, by Victor Sánchez.

> *I talked it over with Dad.*
> *He and I both want you*
> *to have this. It was Mateo's.*
> *But he doesn't need it now.*

"No. I can't. I mean—"

> *Yes, you can. It's been sitting*
> *in a box for four years.*
> *Even if he does come home,*
> *he won't need it.*

"Why are you so nice?"

> *I'm not. Just ask*
> *the Mean Girls Club.*

But She Is Nice

And she makes me laugh.
Oh, yeah, and she can play
killer baseball, too.

I never knew girls
could be all those things
at the same time.

I study the glove,
which is oiled and soft,
but also scarred,
like it's seen a lot of use.

"Hey, Cat. Thanks.
I promise to take good
care of it."

> Better hide it from
> your brother, says Bram.

"No kidding."

> It's sad when you can't
> trust someone you love,
> adds Cat. Believe me. I know.

"Obviously, Mateo played
baseball, and from the looks
of the glove, he played a lot.
So, why did he quit?"

I'm not sure, but I think it was
because of the pressure.
When your father's a major leaguer,
people expect you to be as good.

And he wasn't? asks Bram.

He might have been if he hadn't
given up on it. But honestly,
he didn't want to work that hard.
Not on the field. Not in school.
Mateo was always a little lazy.

"Well, what about you?"

Hey, I'm not lazy!

"No, I was talking about
the pressure. It doesn't seem
to bother you very much."

Because I'm a girl. No one
expects me to play as well
as my dad, or any boy, really.

"And that's okay with you?"

No, but I'm used to it. Anyway,
I like to surprise them. It's fun
to earn a little respect.

She's definitely earned mine.

We're Finishing Lunch

When I happen to look up
and see Will headed toward
the parking lot. Midday?
Is something wrong?

"Be right back. Watch
my stuff, okay?"

I sprint as fast as I can,
catch him just as he reaches
his car. "Where are you going?"

*Home, I guess. I just got
a three-day suspension.*

"For what?"

*He shrugs. There was
a little problem in the hall.*

"Like . . . ?"

*This dude called me a crip.
I was getting ready to pop
him one when Mr. Gabriel
happened to come walking by.*

"But . . . but you didn't
hit the guy, right?"

Nope.

"So, then . . . ?"

> Well, Mr. Gabriel called me
> into the office and asked what
> was going on. And then he started
> to lecture me about better ways
> of dealing with anger.
>
> But it was too late. I was really
> upset and I told Mr. Gabriel
> to leave me the bleep alone.
> He didn't much care for that.

Mr. Gabriel is the dean
of boys, and he's pretty cool.
So I'm guessing Will used
a different word besides "bleep."

"So, you're out until Monday?
Does Dad know?"

> Yes, and yes. According to
> Mr. Gabriel, per school
> district regulations,
> a parent has to be notified.

"Was he mad?"

> What do you think?

I Think I'm Glad

Someone other than me
is letting Dad know Will
has a problem.

Or ten.

I'm also happy I don't have
to cover up for him again.
I hate keeping secrets.

Especially from Dad.

Pretty sure this is the first
time Will's been in trouble
at this school.

Maybe Dad will wake up.

But what about Will?
The look in his eyes tells
me he doesn't care at all.

I'd be embarrassed.

I bet Will thinks
it's a three-day vacation.
Five, including the weekend.

"You picking me up after school?"

Guess I'd better, huh?

He Does

But he's an hour late.
Even in the shade
it's probably ninety degrees.
Hard to work on homework
when you sweat all over it.

I'm just about to call Dad
when Will swerves off
the main drag and weaves
across the lot to where
I'm sitting, all alone.

> *Come on.*
> *Get in.*
> *Let's go.*

His voice is staccato,
his hair is plastered,
wet, around his face,
and B.O. stink drifts
out his open window.

I get in, but leave the door
open. "Dude, have you ever
heard of deodorant?"

> *Hurry up*
> *and shut the door.*

I do, and he punches it.

Will Either Drives

Like he can't find the gas
pedal or like a maniac.
Today, he's going way
too fast for this stretch
of road, and kind of weaving
back and forth.

"Hey, man. Slow down."

                    You gonna make me?

Not me, but turns out
someone's going to,
because behind us
a policeman turns on
his red and blue lights.

                    Oh, man. No way. Here . . .

Will reaches into the center
console, pulls out a bottle
of pills of some kind.

                    Put these in your backpack
                    and don't say a word.

"I can't—"

                    You have to! Hurry up!

Unbelievably, I do.

Will turns on his signal.
Pulls to the far side of the road.
The cop follows, parks.
Gets out of his car.
I hold my breath.
Start to shake.

Chill out.

As the officer approaches,
Will rolls down his window.
The policeman ducks his head.
Looks inside the car.
Studies Will's face.

You in a hurry?

*Yeah. Sorry. We're supposed
to meet our dad and we're late.*

*Better late than never.
Did you realize you were
fifteen miles over the limit?*

*No, I didn't. Guess I wasn't
paying attention. Sorry.*

That's two *sorry*s.

*The cop isn't impressed.
License and registration.*

Good Thing

We're not really in a hurry.
It takes at least twenty minutes
for the policeman to write
Will a speeding ticket.

It's also a good thing
Will gave me the pills
to hold for him, because
his paperwork is in the console
and would've been
directly underneath them.

What isn't a good thing
is that he had them at all.

The officer brings the ticket
back to the car, hands it to Will.
But now he looks at me.

Who are you, young man?

"I'm Trace. Will's brother."

You sure you're his brother?
In Nevada a driver under the age
of eighteen can only carry close
family members as passengers.

"I'm positive I'm his brother."
Why wouldn't he think so?
I sure hope he believes me.

Your court date is June 15.
You'll have to bring a parent
or guardian along and hope
the judge feels like being lenient.
He could suspend your license.

Yikes! Dad's going to be mad.

I understand. Will kind
of chokes on the words.

And slow down. You don't want
to be responsible for hurting
someone, do you? Especially
not your little brother.
That would stay with you forever.

Yes, sir.

Will death-grips the clipboard
the officer hands him.
His shoulders are stiff
with buried rage.
Please don't let it erupt!

But he stuffs it long enough
to sign the ticket, and
the cop says we can leave.

Cautiously

Will puts on his turn signal,
waits for traffic to pass by,
then pulls slowly out
into the right lane.

He checks to make sure
the squad car isn't behind
us, then turns his radio
all the way up and lets out
an ear-blasting curse
before launching a stream
of one-sided "conversation."

I can't believe I got a ticket!
How am I going to pay it?
Dad's gonna be so upset!
What if he takes my car?
What if the judge takes my license?
What am I supposed to do? Walk?

Each question gets him
more worked up.
He talks faster and faster.
And now he's starting
to drive faster.

"Hey, Will. Maybe slow
down a little? I mean—"

Yeah, you're right. Thanks.
It's just, why did this happen?

I probably shouldn't point
out that he's why it happened.

I look out the back window,
see we aren't being followed,
then remove the bottle from
my backpack and give it a shake.

Now I turn down the radio.
"What are these?"

> *Don't worry about them.*
> *They're my prescriptions.*

The label does look like
an honest prescription,
one with Will's name on it, too.

But, "There are two kinds
of pills in here."

> *Right. Because I only want*
> *to carry one bottle with me.*

Sounds logical, except . . .
"Then why were you worried
about the cop seeing them?"

> *Because I didn't want him*
> *to think I was intoxicated.*

Oh, Man

Intoxicated.
I always thought
that meant drunk,
like on beer or whiskey
or something.

Can you get drunk
on pills?

Is that why he drives
so crazy sometimes?

"Are you intoxicated?"

                    Nah. Straight as an arrow.

"So, what do the pills do?"

                    Will huffs, but he answers.
                    One of them is for pain.
                    The other is for depression.

I know a little about
depression because Mom
took medicine for it.

She told me sometimes
the world looked colorless,
and she felt like nothing mattered.

"What color is my shirt?"

He glances over.
I don't know. Purple?

He's messing with me.
My shirt is dark green.
The color of Mr. Cobb's ivy.

"Very funny."

I'm tired of rap, so I change
the station to alternative rock.

This song called "Pain"
is playing. It's by a band
called Three Days Grace,
and the main refrain says
something like it's better
to feel pain than nothing at all.

That's garbage, says Will.

"What do you mean?"

I'm sick and tired of pain.
Believe me, I'd much rather
feel nothing at all.

"You said nothing hurts."

No. I said my face doesn't.

"Yeah. And that you get bad
headaches sometimes."

> *Horrible. Like someone's*
> *hammering nails into my skull.*

"How often do you get them?"

> *Depends. Stress can cause them,*
> *but sometimes they happen*
> *for no reason I can figure out.*

"That's why you take pain pills."

> *Darn straight. They drop*
> *me down into this nice quiet*
> *space where everything's*
> *peaceful and pain-free.*

"But aren't they dangerous?"

> *They can be, I guess.*
> *But not if you're careful.*

"I really hope you're careful.
And I really hope you're all right."

He laughs. A short, loud
bray, like a donkey.

> *I'm fine. Don't I look fine?*

Fact Check

Sometimes he looks fine.
More often, he doesn't.

Sometimes his eyes
are clear, and his words
make sense, and he acts
interested in life—
                    Dad's life
                    my life
                    his own life.

Other times his eyes
don't focus and his words
come out jumbled,
if he says anything at all,
and he doesn't even notice
Dad or me. He just stumbles
like a zombie through
                    Dad's life
                    my life
                    his own life.

And now I wonder
if the pills he's taking
make him be the okay Will
or the one who doesn't
seem to care at all about
                    Dad's life
                    my life
                    his own life.

I Really Want

To talk to Dad, so I'm happy
when he walks in, just as
Will and I finish our tuna
sandwiches and chips dinner.

Will actually made them
and hung out to eat with me.
He used to do stuff like that
all the time, but I've prepared
my own food and eaten alone
for a while now.

Guess having an awful day
made him want to feel
close to his family again?
It would work that way
for me, not that I've ever
been kicked out of school,
and I won't be driving
too fast anytime soon.

It's also strange
for Dad to come home
this early. He must be
worried about Will, too.
He confirms that right away.

> *You almost finished there?*
> *Because you and I need*
> *to talk, Will, and Trace*
> *doesn't need to be involved.*

"I can finish my dinner
outside," I volunteer.

Mostly because if I sit on
the back porch, I'll be able
to hear what they say.

I carry my plate out
the back door, which
I leave cracked just a little.

I don't catch every word,
but it's easy to get the idea.

> Dad: . . . *so disappointed*
> . . . *rely on you*
> . . . *don't understand*
> . . . *can't trust you*

> Will: . . . *sorry, Dad*
> . . . *sorry, Dad*
> . . . *sorry, Dad*
> . . . *won't happen again*

Is that it?
Will got off pretty easy.
Dad says he's grounded,
but how will he know
what Will does when
he's at work or Lily's?

Later On

Will sulks off into his room,
after Dad takes his car keys
away when he finds out
about the ticket.

That gives me the chance
to talk to Dad, who just got
off the phone with Lily.

Trace, my man. What's up?

"I . . . I've been wanting
to talk to you about Will.
I'm worried about him."

*I am, too, son. But you don't
need to. That's my job.*

"But you don't, um . . .
see everything."

Like what?

Will's already in trouble
for school and speeding.
He doesn't need more,
and maybe this will be
his . . . what is it again?

Wake-up call?

Still, I need to know more
about his prescriptions.

"Will takes pills."

>Yes. For his depression.
>You know what that is?

"Like Mom has."

>Right. Their brain chemistry
>is a little off. The pills regulate
>it, make it work more like it should.

"What about the other—"

>Are you talking about me
>behind my back?

Will materializes across
the room like a ghost.
A very upset ghost.

>Your brother is concerned
>about you, Will. That's all.

Will reaches me in three
long strides, gets right up
in my face.

>I told you I'm fine!

I Can Play This

A couple of ways.
I'll try joking first.

"You are so not fine.
Dude, your breath smells
like a dirty aquarium."

His eyes go wide, and he rocks
up on his toes, but then
he gets the tuna reference.

> *Yours smells the same,*
> *with old milk mixed in.*

"Yeah, well yours smells
like far—"

> *That's enough, both of you.*
> *Trace, I'll drive you to and*
> *from school for the rest*
> *of the week, since your brother*
> *is absent a car for a while.*
>
> *I took a few days off.*
> *Not too many, because Lily*
> *and I are planning a really*
> *special summer vacation.*

"Like what?"

> *You'll find out on Friday.*

By Friday

I'm about ready to pop
at the seams, my curiosity
has swollen so much.

Dad wouldn't even give us
a little hint about his big
plans for our summer surprise.

It's been a weird couple
of days, with him home most
of the time. Like, he's fixing
leaky faucets and patching
holes in the walls.

Mostly, he's babysitting Will,
which sounds wrong,
considering how old Will is.
But if any seventeen-year-old
in the universe needs watching,
it's definitely my brother.

I've been kind of distracted
at school. Good thing Cat's been
there to help me focus on
our robotics project and Bram
has been his usual entertaining
self, cracking stupid jokes
whenever I get too serious
or antsy about tonight.

The big reveal is almost here.

Dad Picks Me Up

After school, but instead
of taking me home,
he gets on the freeway.

"Where are we going?"

>   *To pick up your grandpa Russ.*

"Really?" Even though
he lives pretty close,
we don't see him very often.

>   *Yeah. He's coming to dinner,*
>   *and his car's in the shop.*
>   *I thought it was about time*
>   *we spent an evening together.*

"Why has it been so long?"

>   *Good question. I guess because*
>   *I've been so focused on work.*

He doesn't say, "and Lily,"
but the thought hangs in
the air between us.

>   *It feels like I haven't made*
>   *enough time for you and Will,*
>   *let alone my father. But we can*
>   *change that. I want to.*

"Sounds good, Dad."

It does.

I hope he means it.
I hope he follows through.
I hope he finds a way
to make more time
for Will and me.

But I worry
our family's too broken.

I worry
that even if we change
for the better,
it won't mean
everything will be solid.

I worry
that the more we try
to put ourselves back
together, the farther
apart we'll end up.

I worry
if Dad gives too much
of his love to Lily,
it will mean he has less
love for Will and me.

Desert Sky Retirement Village

Is a pretty big place—
blocks and blocks
of plain little homes
with yards that aren't
too much work for older people,
all behind a big fence
to keep everyone safe.

Most of them probably
own cars, but they drive
around their neighborhoods,
to the pool or tennis or
shuffleboard courts, in golf carts.

Speaking of shuffleboard.
"Lily's coming tonight, right?"

> *Yes, of course.*

"Couldn't she have driven
Grandpa instead of us
picking him up?"

> *She was off today. Spent*
> *most of it at the house.*

"Our house?"

> *Yes, our house. Working*
> *on a fabulous dinner.*

Cooking in her kitchen
is one thing. Cooking
in ours is another.
Even if her food *is* good.
It feels like a . . . violation.
I think that's the right word.

Dad winds through the street
maze, dodging golf carts
and dog walkers. I'm not
sure how he knows where
to turn, but this way, then
that way, finally he pulls
up in front of Grandpa's.

>   *He's expecting us. Want*
>   *to go ring the bell?*

I do.
Grandpa comes to the door.
He's not alone.
Why is this familiar?

>   *Trace! So great to see you.*
>   *Oh. This is my friend Clara.*
>   *Clara, this is my grandson.*

Seriously? Grandpa has
a girlfriend, too?

I Learn All About Clara

On our drive home.
She and Grandpa met
at the pool four months ago.
They both play golf.
Neither likes shuffleboard.

She's a "divorcée."
I guess that means
she and her husband
got divorced. Not that
I need the details.

She has three grown kids—
two daughters and a son—
and seven grandkids.
They all live in Chicago,
where she's from, but Clara
prefers the Vegas weather,
so they'll have to come visit her here.

> *A warm-weather lover.*
> *We have something*
> *in common,* says Dad.

> *Two things,* corrects Grandpa.
> *Don't forget about me!*

Grandpa does most
of the talking, which
is normal. Clara is quiet
but smiles a lot. She's okay.

Everything's okay.
Well, mostly.

Everything's fine.
Kind of.

Everything's different.
For sure.

What would it take
to make everything
like it was?

If I could go back in time,
stop Will from playing that night,
where would we be today?

Would we live
in our old house,
go to our old school?

Would it be Mom
in the kitchen,
working on dinner?

Or would life
just have thrown us
different curveballs?

There's Another Surprise

Waiting for me at home.
It greets me at the front door,
holding a ball in its mouth.

"Sylvester!"

My first thought is *Sweet!*
My second is we've never
had a dog in this house,
or any kind of animal.

Does this mean something?

Oh, well. He wants to play,
and I'm game, so we go
out into the backyard.

Mr. Cobb hears us and sticks
his face over the fence.

New dog?

"He belongs to Dad's friend.
Just visiting." For now, anyway.

Thought you were coming
over to do some yardwork?

"Oh, man. Sorry. Some
stuff happened. Maybe Sunday?
I have a game tomorrow."

Did you get hold of a glove?

"Yeah. A teammate had
an extra. I'll still take care
of your ivy, though."

It'll be here when you get
here. Hey, I'd like to watch
you play ball. You pitch, right?
See if you're as good as Koufax.

I laugh and tell him where
the field is located and
what time to get there.

I toss the ball a few more
times for Sylvester, then
we go inside to enjoy
the magnificent feast
Dad talked about.

He and Lily are in the kitchen,
which smells really, really good.
I think maybe she baked bread
or rolls or something with yeast.

Dad says it will still be fifteen
minutes until we can eat,
and to go watch TV with
Grandpa and Clara.

They're Tuned In

To one of those entertainment
programs. The kind with more
gossip than information.

It's a commercial when I sit
down on the chair next to
the sofa where Grandpa
and Clara are sitting,
knee-touching-knee
and holding hands.

It's weird enough seeing
Dad and Lily acting like
that. But my grandfather?

Yikes!

The show comes back on,
and the announcer says,

> And now, in the music world,
> there's a new power couple
> coming to a venue near you.
> Rumor has it they met at
> a Vail ski resort in February.

"Hey, Will!" I yell. "Come here!"

On camera, for everyone
(including me) to see, is my mom.
She's singing into a microphone.

And so is a guy with super-
long hair. The same microphone.
He looks familiar, but I'm not
sure exactly who he is until
the announcer tells me,

> *Serene Etienne and Rory Davis*
> *are making beautiful music*
> *together, both on- and offstage.*

Rory Davis sings lead for
a hard rock band. Apparently,
he and Mom are a "thing."

> Will wanders in. *What?*

"Check it out."

Will turns outrageously red
eyes toward the TV. He sniffs.

> *Yeah, so?*

"Did you know?"

> *No, but I'm not surprised.*

> *. . . will be on tour together*
> *this summer,* continues
> the announcer. *They plan*
> *both US and European dates.*

My Mouth Falls Open

Why didn't Mom say anything
about him when I talked to her?

If they met in February,
they've been together for a while.

Why did she make me believe
we might spend time together?

If they're planning a huge tour,
that isn't going to happen.

"I can't believe it."

I can, says Will.

What? asks Clara.

Serene is their mother,
explains Grandpa.

"If she ever remembers."

She doesn't, says Will.
Not for a long, long time.

He turns on one heel,
goes back to his bedroom.

Just as Dad calls us to dinner.

I've Lost My Appetite

Not even the fresh-from-the-oven
homemade bread, roasted pernil
(roast pork) with adobo, or sweet plantains
leaking delicious-smelling steam
in the middle of the table can fix that.

Will doesn't want to leave his room
but Dad insists. He and I sit silently
while everyone else passes plates
and chatters about how good Lily's
first attempt at Puerto Rican food
(Dad's favorite!) is. I feel as low
as Will looks. But there's something
else about him. Something off.

And I don't think it has anything
to do with Mom and Rory Davis.
It's like he doesn't dare look anyone
in the eye. Shoulders hunched over,
he stares down at his empty plate.

> *What's with all the doom
> and gloom?* asks Dad.

I say nothing.
Will says nothing.
Clara says nothing.

> Finally, Grandpa says,
> way too calmly, *Serene
> was on the television.*

I Jump In

"Yeah! She's going on
an extended tour.
With her new boyfriend
and his stupid band.

"This summer. After she leaves
Tahoe. When she told me
she'd try to come visit!"

> *Whoa*, says Dad. *Take it easy.
> I never heard anything about
> a possible summer visit.*

> *That's because he made it all
> up in his head*, argues Will.

"Nuh-uh. She totally did!
Also that we might go see
Maureen and Paul in Colorado."

> *She hasn't mentioned it
> to me*, says Dad. *When did
> you talk to her about it?*

"A few days ago."

> *You must've called her.*

> *Duh*, says Will.

"Who cares?"

*Does it really matter who
called who?* Lily interrupts.
*I'm sorry if your mom
disappointed you, Trace.
I'm sure she'll make it up to you.*

I wouldn't count on it,
says Will. *Not her thing.*

Please pass the bread,
requests Grandpa.

Dad clears his throat. *I wish
you boys would eat. Lily
worked extremely hard
preparing this meal.*

I take a piece of bread
when it passes by me.
Stuff a huge bite in my mouth.
Chew. Chew. Chew. Swallow.

"This is good, Lily."

Maybe I'm a little hungry
after all. I ask for some pernil
and plantains, too.

Why not? Maybe food
can take the edge off.
I don't want to hurt.

Will Pretends to Pick

At a few bites, too.

Clara and Lily eat
like polite ladies—slowly,
chewing every mouthful
a whole lot of times.

Dad and Grandpa chow down.
Not, like, gross. But at
a steady pace. And they
both ask for seconds.

But while Dad eats, he keeps
an eye on Will and me,
like he's waiting for stuff
to blow up again, not
that I blame him.

> Finally, he asks Lily,
> *Should we share our*
> *surprise with the boys?*

> *I think we should.*
> *You tell them.*

> *We haven't had a real*
> *vacation in a long time.*
> *Lily has a lot of contacts,*
> *and she managed to set us*
> *up with an amazing trip. . . .*

No Way!

I can't believe it!
After school gets out
for summer, we're rafting
the Colorado River down
through the Grand Canyon.

Well, we won't do the whole
length. Instead, we'll fly in a small
plane to this ranch where
we can ride horses and ATVs.

Then we'll helicopter to a place
closer to Vegas and get on
a raft for two whole days,
camping along the way.

"Seriously, Dad?"

> *Would I kid you about*
> *something like that?*

I want to go! says Grandpa.

> *We can probably arrange*
> *it, says Lily. But we'd have*
> *to do it right away. It's one*
> *of the most popular trips.*
> *People come from all over*
> *the world to enjoy it.*

Lukewarm

That's what I'd call
Will's reaction.
His eyes don't even lift
off his plate while Lily
gives all the exciting details.
Look at all the rides we get:
Small plane.
Helicopter.
Horseback.
ATV.

And that's all before
we even strap into the big
raft for whitewater running
and slow-water floating.
I mean, come on!

Grandpa and Clara are excited.
Dad and Lily are excited.
I can barely hold my excitement
inside. How can I wait until June?

But Will just sits there until
finally he opens his mouth.

Aren't there any, like,
age requirements?

Minimum age of eight.
The rafts are powered,
so no one has to paddle.

No maximum age cutoff,
I hope, says Grandpa.

> *No, not as long as you're*
> *in good health. I think*
> *you and Clara are fine.*
> *Anyway, even if there was,*
> *you two aren't all that old.*

Grandpa's in his sixties.
That's pretty darn old.
But he's still in decent shape.
And I guess Clara looks okay, too.

Still, I tease, "You better go
to the gym, Grandpa.
Get buffed. You've got time."

> *Oof. I shouldn't have to point*
> *this out, young man, but I go*
> *to the gym on the regular.*

He pumps his arm muscles,
and I have to admit a lot
of people would admire his biceps.
Especially old people.

"Okay, Gramps. Guess you
can come along."

Everyone looks happy.
Except Will.

After Dessert

Which is made-from-scratch
tres leches cake with vanilla ice cream,
the chef (that would be Lily) volunteers
to drive Grandpa and Clara home.

*Sylvester will take the front
seat, of course. But only if
you two promise to be good
in the back,* she jokes.

Define "good," answers
Grandpa, and now I wonder
why we haven't had him over
more. He's the kind of funny
our family needs. So is Lily.

As for Sylvester, he's been
super good the whole time.
No fur anywhere.
No mess on the carpet.
No barking at inappropriate times.
Thinking I need to ask Dad
for a dog again. Sylvester
can be his role model.
Do dogs even have those?

As soon as they're gone,
Will (who didn't even try
the tres leches, and I don't think
noticed the dog) stands up
wordlessly and hits his room.

I help Dad finish cleaning
up the kitchen. My brain
is churning so many questions
and ideas, I don't know
where to start with them.

But two things weigh
more than the others.

"Hey, Dad. Why didn't Mom
tell me about Rory Davis
when I talked to her?"

>He sighs. *I can't say for sure,*
>*but I think maybe she didn't*
>*want to hurt you. Sort of like*
>*when I first started seeing Lily.*

"I told her about you and Lily."

>*You did? What did she say?*

"That it's good you found
someone special and that
nobody wants to be alone."

>*Well, she's mostly right about*
>*that. I've met a few content*
>*loners in my day, but not many.*

That Makes Me Think

When we moved across town
and I started Rainbow Ridge,
the only reason I had friends
was because of Little League.

But there are a couple of kids
at school who are always
alone, and they never
look happy. It must be hard
not to have any friends.

And what about Mr. Cobb?
No wonder he's always
peeking over the fence
when he hears us outside.

Right after we came here,
I thought he was annoying.
Sometimes I still think he is.
But if I take the time to listen
to his stories, they can be
interesting, like the one
he told me a few days ago.

"Hey, Dad. Did you know
Mr. Cobb was in the army
and fought in Vietnam?"

> *Really? No, I didn't know*
> *about that. But where did*
> *the question come from?*

"I was thinking about loners,
since you mentioned them.
Do you supposed he was
ever married? Or has kids?"

*I couldn't say. Maybe you
should ask him sometime.*

Maybe I should.
Maybe on Sunday.
While I weed his ivy.

But now someone else
crosses my mind.

"Hey, Dad. What about Will?"

Dad grins. *He's never been
married and I don't think
he has any kids. I hope not.*

"Ha-ha. No. I mean . . ."
I glance over my shoulder
to make sure Will's not lurking.
"He's kind of a loner."

He has friends, doesn't he?

"He used to. But I'm not
sure the people he hangs
out with are really his friends."

As Soon as the Words

Leave my mouth,
I realize they're true.
If he had real friends,
we'd see them once
in a while. We never do.
And just because he leaves
the house doesn't mean
he's chilling with buddies.

"He wasn't very excited
about the rafting trip."

I noticed. My guess is
he's afraid of getting hurt.

"But if little kids can do
it, and if Will wears a helmet,
it's probably safe, right?"

For the most part. That's why
we chose this one in particular.
Of course, any physical activity
carries some amount of risk.

But I wouldn't put your brother
in harm's way, and I'm hoping
the experience will help him find
a little self-confidence again.

I hope so, too.
I still want the old Will back.

But It's the New Will

Who rides along to my game.
Dad insists that he come,
even though he doesn't want
to, and that makes him mad.

> *Stop being so belligerent,*
> *Dad finally tells him.*

> *Little League games stink.*
> *You've seen one, you've seen*
> *them all. Not even real baseball.*

That stings. "Little League
is too real baseball.
Like you'd know, anyway."

> *How are you going to play*
> *without a mitt?* Will sneers.

"I've got a *glove*. Not that
you care." I struggle
not to call him a thief.

> *That's enough, Will.*
> *Trace works hard to be*
> *the best he can at this game.*
> *The least you can do is support him.*

> *This is not how I want*
> *to spend my Saturday.*

I Want to Yell

Want to tell him
watching him play
football was never
my idea of a fun
Friday night.

Want to tell him
high school football
is nothing like *real*
football, and *real*
players never get hurt.

Want to tell him
I'm sick of
                    his meanness
        sick of
                    his lies
        sick of
                    his self-pity
        sick of

        him
                telling Dad
                telling Mom
                telling me

                    we don't deserve
                            his respect
                            his trust
                            his love.

Instead

I clamp my mouth shut.

Stare out the window.

Watch the blur of sky to mountaintops.

Tune out my dad, who's doing his best

       to make me know he's proud of me.

We bump down the road we drive on

       almost every day, sometimes twice.

The neighborhoods, stores, and

       churches and schools look the same.

Beyond them, the same desert

       stretches to familiar hills and peaks.

For as long as I can remember,

       this place has been my home.

I've never felt unsafe biking these

       streets or walking on these sidewalks.

But I'm scared for my brother.

Problem Is

Too much thinking
messes up my focus.
Coach Hal's pep talk
goes in one ear,
straight out the other.

I try to find it again
by concentrating on
the feel of my new
used glove. It's like
it was made for my hand.

Worse, I think my focus
problem is contagious.
Coach Tom started Cat on
the mound. She's pitching
wild—in the dirt, past
the catcher. The other team
scores three runs in the first.

Second inning, she loads
the bases with no outs.
Coach Tom waves me in,
and as he starts walking
toward the mound,
there's no way to miss
Will, yelling from the stands.

What's wrong with you?
Stupid girls can't pitch!

Every head snaps
in Will's direction.
Coaches. Players.
Parents, siblings,
random others.

That includes my dad
and Mr. Cobb, who's sitting
a few seats away.

Also, Cat's father,
her brother, and a lady,
not Victor Sánchez's
personal assistant,
who's right there with them.

I want to give Cat a hug,
but before I can even reach
the mound, she stomps
toward the dugout,
more angry than hurt.
At least that's what her
body language screams.

I should go get in Will's face.
Should ask what's wrong
with him, and why he always
has to be so awful. Should tell
him Cat has more talent in
her little toe than he ever did.

But Coach Tom

Is calling for me to pitch.
Coach Hal has convinced Cat
to catch, and sent Bram
out to play first base.

Meanwhile, Dad is hauling
Will out of the stands,
which is probably good,
because Victor Sánchez
looks ready to do it for him.

And I don't blame him.

We desperately try to get
back in the game, but
there's no possible way
that will happen.

I pitch okay, but the three
on-base runners all score,
and it's six to nothing.

The other team either
feels sorry for us or their
focus is broken, too,
because they don't extend
their six-run lead.

We manage to score two,
and that's the game.

We high-five the other team,
and Coach gives us the ol'
"you can't win 'em all" speech.

Then I go over to Cat, who
still looks shook. "I'm sorry
about my brother. He can be
a real jer—"

>*It's not him.* She sounds
>like she's going to cry.

"Then what is it?"

She wags her head toward
where her family is sitting.

>*My mom got here last night.*
>*My brother was with some bad*
>*people and got arrested.*

>*Mom wants Dad to pay for*
>*a lawyer to get him out*
>*of jail, but Dad doesn't want to.*

"Why not?"

>*He says Mateo needs to learn*
>*a lesson so maybe he'll turn*
>*his life around and do better.*

Whoa

Seems kind of harsh.
I wonder if it's the right
thing to do.

"What do you think?"

> *I don't know. Mom and Dad*
> *argued about it for a long*
> *time, so I heard both sides.*
> *I kind of think Dad's right.*
>
> *It's not that I want Mateo*
> *to stay in jail, but if he keeps*
> *going in a bad direction,*
> *who knows what he might do?*

"What if jail just makes
him worse?"

> *You sound like Mom.*
> *That's exactly what she said.*

"What did your dad say?"

> *He said it would be hard*
> *to get worse than carjacking.*

"What's that?"

> *Stealing cars when their drivers*
> *are still sitting in them.*

Oh. Like in the movies.
Sometimes the bad guys
grab the drivers and yank
them right out of their cars.

Sometimes . . . "Mateo
didn't use a gun, did he?"

> *No. But he had one.*
> *At least, the cops found*
> *one under the seat.*
> *He swears it isn't his, but . . .*

That's what they all say.
Just like in the movies.

Bram is sitting nearby,
close enough to have
overheard our conversation.
He's shaking his head in a slow
back-and-forth roll.

That's pretty much how I feel.
And all I can say at this point
is "Sorry, Cat."

> *Yeah. Me, too. Better go.*

Thanks to Will

I'm riding home with Mr. Cobb.
When he sees me looking
around for Dad, who's nowhere
in sight, he waves me over.

> *Your father thought it best*
> *that he and your brother leave.*
> *You don't mind coming with me?*

"No. Why would I?"

> *Some people think old farts*
> *like me can't drive very well.*

"Guess I'll find out."

> *Guess you will.*

I follow him to the parking
lot. I have no idea what
he drives. His car is always
parked in his garage, and
I never see him go anywhere.

> *Over here.*

"No way! That's your car?"

> *You ever ridden in a Corvette?*

"Uh, no."

Well, get on in. This baby
is a 1972 classic, and boy,
does she get up and go!

"Don't get a ticket, okay?"

He laughs and we buckle up.
The car smells like old leather,
though it isn't cracked or anything.
He must take excellent care of it.

When Mr. Cobb starts the engine,
it growls to life, then rumbles.

"Have you had her for a long time?"

>*Since she rolled off the line.*
>*Becky is the love of my life.*
>*Well, there was one other.*

I wait for a minute, but
when he doesn't offer more
info, I go ahead and ask,
"Who was the other one?"

>*My wife. Leona and I were*
>*married forty-four years.*
>*She's been gone for three,*
>*and I miss her every day.*
>*Together we drove ol' Becky*
>*here all around the US of A.*

Mr. Cobb

Doesn't drive fast enough
to get a ticket. For a while.

You in a hurry to get home?

"Not really. It's probably
pretty tense around there."

*Ahem. Well, if you don't mind,
I'd like to take Becky for a run
on the freeway. She needs
to sprint every now and again.*

"Cool."
As in super cool.

Moth wings flutter in my stomach
when he merges onto the interstate,
takes a deep peek in his rearview mirror.

Hang on to your hat!

We accelerate like a bullet.
Two seconds takes us from sixty mph
to . . . I have no idea. I steal a glance
at the speedometer.

70

80

90

100

Mr. Cobb lifts his foot.

> *That oughta do it. Gotta blow*
> *the garage sludge out of her pipes.*
> *She wasn't meant to retire.*
> *Makes her downright testy.*

That was the most thrilling
few minutes of my whole
life! I wonder if . . .

"Hey, Mr. Cobb. Did you ever
raft the Colorado River?"

> *Sure. Three times. Why?*

I tell him about our summer
plans. "I'm excited, but also
a little worried. Do you think
it's okay for Will?"

> *You mean because of his TBI?*
> *Leona and I did the whole length*
> *of the canyon, and there's a lot*
> *more whitewater upriver from*
> *the stretch you'll be on.*
>
> *Accidents aren't impossible,*
> *but they're rare, especially on*
> *the powered rafts. The guides*
> *know their stuff. He'll be fine.*

We Exit

The freeway and Mr. Cobb zigzags
through the surface streets,
observing the speed limits.

Still, heads turn when the cherry-red
'Vette drives by, and it sort of feels
like being a celebrity or something.

Like Victor Sánchez.
Like Rory Davis.
Like Serene Etienne (aka Mom).

The last thought makes me
shrivel inside,
a worm on hot asphalt.

"I wish we would've played
better today," I say.

>	All teams have off days,
>	and considering your start,
>	you didn't finish so bad.

"Yeah. Poor Cat. She's usually
a great pitcher, but bad stuff's
going on with her brother.
She was kind of distracted."

>	Ah. And how about your brother?

"You got a hint today."

Did you talk to your dad
about your concerns?

"A little. And my mom, too.
They mostly think
it's regular teenager stuff."

Well, maybe it is, and maybe
it's more, but at least
you tried to let them know.

He turns into his driveway,
opens the garage door
with a remote in the car.

Mind helping me wipe her off?

"Not if I can have another
ride in Becky sometime."
We use special dusters.
Then Mr. Cobb puts Becky
to bed (that's what he calls
it) beneath her custom cover.

"Thanks, Mr. C. I'll come over
tomorrow and weed your ivy."

Thanks for your company.
It gets lonely around here.

I understand. I get lonely, too.

Home Again

And when I open the door,
I hit a wall of silence.
I expected maybe yelling
or hardcore lecturing
at the very least.

"Hey! Where is everyone?"

> Dad stomps into view in the hall.
> *Grab a shower and dress nice.*
> *We're going out to dinner.*

"With Lily?"

> *No, just you and me.*

"What about Will?"

> *He went out the window*
> *right after we got home.*

"Did you give him his keys?"

> *Nope. He left on foot, unless*
> *someone picked him up.*

"So why are we going dinner?"

> *Because you didn't escape*
> *through the window, and*
> *because I don't feel like cooking.*

Dad Lets Me Choose

Where I want to eat.
I could say Steak 'n Shake,
but I'm in the mood
for something else.
"Can we have sushi?"

Your choice, like I said.

We go to our favorite
place, and Dad lets me get
the all-you-can-eat. I'm not
so big on straight raw fish,
but I like the rolls a lot.

"We lost the game," I say.

You had a rough start.

"Yeah. Cat couldn't focus.
She found out her brother
is in jail for carjacking."

Dad whistles quietly.
That's tough. I'm surprised.
He comes from a good home.

"Yeah, well, so does Will."

I hope so. I try to do right
by you boys. This isn't all
Will's fault, though. He—

"Stop making excuses
for him. It's his *choice*
to get into trouble.
It's his *choice* to drive
too fast or to ditch school . . ."

Oops. I never mentioned
that to Dad.

> *What do you mean, ditch?*
> *That's not why he's suspended.*

"Well, it was one day, and
he told me he was sick, and
he did puke in the parking lot, and—"

> *I never heard anything about*
> *him getting sick and leaving school.*

Yeah, that's what I figured.
But I'm not going to say so.
"Sorry. Thought you knew."

> *Hey, Trace. Anytime you think*
> *there's a problem, whether*
> *with Will or with you, please*
> *come to me, okay? I can't fix*
> *anything if I'm left in the dark.*

I'm Starting to Think

I can't fix everything
all on my own. That maybe
it might take Dad and me
working together.

Suddenly, I remember
that Will interrupted me
that day I wanted to ask
Dad about his medications.

"Hey, Dad. You know when
we talked about the pills Will takes?"

He nods. *For his depression.*

"What about the other ones?"

What other ones?

"The pain pills he takes."

You mean like aspirin?

"No. I don't know what
they are, except not aspirin."

*His only meds I'm aware
of are the antidepressants.
What makes you think
he takes pain pills?*

"I saw them. That day
he got the ticket. He told
me they're for the awful
headaches he gets sometimes."

Dad gives a low whistle,
and his forehead creases.

> *I know he used to get headaches,*
> *but he hasn't said anything about*
> *them lately. Are you sure about this?*

"One hundred percent!"

> *It's been a while since he's*
> *seen his doctor, too. Guess I'd*
> *better make an appointment.*
> *Thanks for the nudge, Trace.*

"I just want him to be
okay. And I don't want
you to be in the dark."

> *That makes two of us, son.*

But the Reason

It's going to be hard
becomes clear before long.

We're almost home
when Dad spies Will
walking in that direction.
He pulls against the sidewalk.

Want a ride?

Will looks confused.
Spacy, even. His eyes
are unfocused, and it seems
to take several seconds
for him to recognize us.

Dad checks him out,
and I think he understands
that this is the Will I worry about.

Will? You solid?

Sure, Dad.

*Great. So do you want a ride
or don't you? PS: Say okay.*

Uh . . . I guess so.

Will slides into the back seat,
slumps, closes his eyes.

Dad looks in the rearview
mirror and takes note.

>*We had sushi for dinner,* he says.
Missed you being there.

>*It's okay. I'm not hungry.*

>*Headache?*

Pretty sure Will's glaring
at the back of my skull.

>*Not at the moment,* he says.

>*Why haven't you mentioned
them? They're worrisome.*

>*No big deal. I've got them
under control.*

"Will! You said—"

>*You keep out of this or I'll—*

>*That's enough, Will,* barks Dad.
*We'll get you in to see your doctor.
Meanwhile, what about these
pain pills Trace mentioned?*

>Will snorts. *You mean Motrin?*

You Can Buy

Motrin at the store.
It's sort of like aspirin.
I don't think that's what
I saw in the prescription
bottle with Will's antidepressants.

But I'm pretty sure
Will's already mad at me,
so I keep my mouth shut.
Besides, how would
I really know?

Well, please be careful, says
Dad. *Too much of that stuff
can mess up your gut.*

We wouldn't want that.

Dad does not appreciate
Will's snarky comeback.
His arms tense and his hands
tighten around the steering wheel.

Where have you been, by the way?

Nowhere. Walking around.

For almost three hours?

Better than arguing with you.

Which Leads To

An awful argument
as soon as they get home.

They're barely across
the threshold when
Dad throws the first
grenade, which happens
to be about ditching school.

> I hear you think attending
> school is discretionary. It's not.

I suffer Will's evil stare,
but as soon as he launches
his counterattack, I decide
I don't want to listen.

> My brother has a big mouth.
> I don't suppose he told you
> I was feeling sick that day?

> Why didn't you go to the nurse?
> Or at least let the office know?

> I didn't think they'd want
> me to puke all over their floor.

I rush down the hall
to my room. Close the door.
Turn on my music.
Plug in my headphones.

That mostly disguises
their ugly words until
they move into the hall
outside my bedroom
and yell so loudly
that not even heavy,
metal can drown
them all the way out.

It's like a tennis match
of words, and not nice ones.

thoughtless

selfish

incorrigible

heartless

punk

idiot

It goes on for a very
long time, and it's almost
enough to make me want
to escape out my window.

It's Gray Outside

When I wake the next morning.
Spring rain is rare in Vegas,
but it sure looks like the skies
might open up and pour.

It hasn't started yet, though,
so I jump up and get dressed.
No one's in the kitchen,
and I doubt Dad or Will
would care if I skip breakfast.

I leave a note on the counter:
Doing chores for Mr. Cobb.
It's not quite eight, and he
might be asleep, but I know
where the garden tools are.

I'm only a little surprised
to find him drinking coffee
on his front porch. "Morning!
Figured I'd better get to work
in case it decides to rain."

> *Sure looks like it could.*
> *Wouldn't that be a blessing?*

Even the clouds are a blessing
because it's not too hot.
Still, the work is hard, and
before too long I'm sweating.

After an Hour or So

Mr. Cobb brings me a cold
tumbler of water.

>   *Thought you could use this.*

I gulp down half the glass,
and he looks over the large
pile of weeds I've pulled.

>   *You're doing good work, son.*

"Thanks. Hey, Mr. C. I've been
thinking . . ." I have, actually.
About Mateo and Will, and
what might happen to them.

"You know when you went
to Vietnam? I know the war
was bad, but was there anything
good about joining the army?"

>   *Well, yes. I trained to be a medic.*
>   *My job was to keep fallen soldiers*
>   *alive until the evac helicopters*
>   *could arrive and get them out.*

>   *After the war, the army put me*
>   *through college and helped*
>   *me become a civilian nurse.*

"You were a nurse?"

He laughs. *Oh, yes. A good*
one, too. Maybe not as pretty
as some of the lady nurses.

But that was my job for thirty
years. My Leona was a nurse, too.
In fact, we met at the hospital
where we both were employed.
As some people say, the good
Lord works in mysterious ways.

I don't know about that,
but if it's even a possibility,
I sure hope the good Lord's
mysterious ways can help
my brother. Mateo, too.

I go back to work.
The weed pile grows.

Next, I clip back the ivy
where it crawls too close
to the grass. I'm still trimming
when it starts to rain.

Fat drops soak the soil,
and I smell wet desert.
People who don't know
what that means should.

It means life.

I Learned That

From Dad, and I remember
exactly when he told me.

It was the night Will got hurt.
We were at the hospital,
and he and I took a little walk
outside. The moon was almost
hidden by a big bank of clouds.

> Looks like it's going to rain,
> Dad said. Smell it coming?

I sniffed the air, which
was thick with moisture.
That's really obvious
in the bone-dry desert.
"Yeah. It's almost here."

> Your grandma Isabel
> always said rain is life.
> I grew up on a farm
> in Minnesota, as you know.
>
> We relied on rain to make
> our fields grow, and that corn
> and wheat and beans fed people.
> Drought years decimated crops.
>
> When I was little, I used to wonder
> how many other kids went hungry
> when the rain didn't come.

That was the first time
I really thought about food
in the grocery store being grown
somewhere like Minnesota.

It was probably the first time
I pictured Dad as a boy, too.
I knew about the farm, but
he hardly ever talked about it,
or his mother, who gave him
his "Puerto Rican good looks."

"Do you miss Grandma Isabel?"

> *Sure. She was my mom.*
> *How could I not miss her?*
>
> *Now, she wasn't real happy*
> *about me throwing my stuff*
> *in a backpack and moving*
> *out here to Vegas. She swore*
> *I'd come running home in a month.*

"But you didn't."

> *No. I've never regretted that.*
> *But I do wish I'd gone back*
> *to visit more before she passed.*
> *You always think you'll have*
> *plenty of time, but sometimes*
> *life throws you curveballs.*

That Made Me Sad Then

And it makes me sad now.
Because it reminds
me of Mom.

I don't guess Will and I
are going to die anytime
soon, but what if one of us
did, and she never came
to visit before it happened?

Would she even feel bad?
Would she wish she'd made
different decisions?

What if something bad
happened to her?

It isn't my choice
not to see her.
She's the one
who's staying away.

What if she died today?

I'd be crushed
because I love her.
But I think I'd hate
her just a little.

And I'm not sure
I could ever forgive her.

The Rain Starts to Fall Harder

I keep working until
I'm soaked and my muscles
are tired of squatting
and pulling and carrying
sopping piles of yard
waste to the compost bin.

Finally, Mr. Cobb calls me
over to the porch. Guess
he doesn't want to get wet.

> *It's past lunchtime, and you*
> *look like you could use dry*
> *clothes. Here's an IOU until*
> *my check gets here.*

I look at the piece of paper.
"Thirty dollars?"
That's more than usual.

> *You deserve it.*

I don't guess Will would
borrow an IOU, but when
Mr. C gives me the money,
I'll need a new place to stash it.
I'll have to think about that.

> *Now go on. Get some lunch.*
> *But first, change your clothes.*
> *You don't want to get sick.*

I Don't Get Sick

Which is good, because the next
few weeks are really busy.

Little League ramps up
because the season will
end soon, and we want
to play in the regionals.

We're practicing extra.
Working twice as hard.
And it's really, really hot.
But no one complains.

In school, it's year-end
testing, which isn't too bad.
I know most of the answers,
think I'll earn high scores.

Cat and I have built our robot.
One of the challenges at the big
event requires throwing
objects at targets, which
is exactly what we designed
our Strike 'Em Out bot to do.

The trick now is getting
the programming exactly
right, and that's what we're
currently working on.
I'm glad Cat's my partner.
She's super good at this.

At Home

Things have been mostly
quiet, at least when
it comes to Will.

No fights.
No arguments.
No real trouble.

He's been good
about transportation.
Hasn't made me late.
Hasn't left me stranded.

I also doubt in all this time
he's said more than a hundred
words altogether to Dad and me.

He hangs out in his room.
Plays video games, and
sometimes I hear him talking
on his phone. Not sure to who.

He's easier to get along with
mostly because he avoids
confrontation.

But I don't think
that makes him
all right.

What Really Worries Me

Is the rafting trip.
Not the trip itself.
I can hardly wait!

But the way Will refuses
to participate in the planning.

It's so fun!
Dad and Lily have made
a big list of stuff we'll need.

We don't have to worry
about things like tents
or sleeping bags. The tour
company provides them.

But we'll want
to bring

        sunscreen
        swim shirts and shorts
        beach towels
        reading materials
        seasick patches
        UV-resistant sunglasses
        straps for our sunglasses
        waterproof bags for our

                phones
                towels
                extra clothes
                prescriptions

Prescriptions. Yeah.

But Even

If Will doesn't care
about any of that,
he should be interested
in the videos Lily shares.

Most are of the Colorado
above where we'll actually be,
but man, are they thrilling!
One day, I'll do those crazier
stretches of the river, too.

We're actually lucky
because we live in Vegas.
Most people who run the Colorado
down the Grand Canyon
have to make their way
to Las Vegas first.

This is where most river-
rafting trips begin and finish.

The tour companies
pick you up at a Vegas hotel.
Then you drive or fly
to the far end, where
you "embark."
That means get on
board the raft.

These aren't little rafts.
They're big, like thirty-five

feet long, and they hold
fifteen people, plus all the gear.
You sit on these padded
pontoons, and down
the river you go.

There are lots of other
rivers in lots of different
places you can raft like this.
But the Grand Canyon
is really special.
And instead of looking
down into it,
you're looking up
out of it toward the rim.

The water is beautiful.
Kind of turquoise and white.
The rapids are rowdy.
But there are quiet stretches, too.
The canyon walls are steep.
Red and gray and purple layers,
and locked in them are all kinds of fossils.

The more we learn
about the trip, the more
excited I get. But the more
I mention it, the more
Will withdraws.
I wish he'd get excited, too.

The Night Before

Our last Little League game,
I stay over at Bram's.
His mom makes homemade
pizza, and I'm not talking
about the frozen kind.

We watch *A League of Their Own*
on TV, to get us in the mood.
Whole teams of girls playing
baseball! Bram's dad says
it's a fictional story, but
the women's league was real.

"Can you believe it?" I ask.

> *It was only because of the war,*
> says Bram. *When the soldiers*
> *came home, they quit playing.*

"I know. And it probably
wouldn't happen today,
because girls can be soldiers,
too. I guess they can do
anything boys can, huh?"

> *Nah. They couldn't wrestle*
> *Jack Swagger, I bet.*

Jack Swagger is a professional
wrestling superstar, and he's huge.
"Okay, maybe not. So, *almost* anything."

I don't know about all girls.
Some of them are pretty useless.

I think about Leah and Sara
and Star, who seem kind of *useless*.
But I don't really know them.
Maybe they could play baseball
if they wanted to. As if they would.

"Well, Cat isn't. I kind of hope
Coach Tom starts her tomorrow."

You mean pitching?
Don't you want to start?

"When Cat's on, she might
be better than me, and
we have to win tomorrow
to get into the playoffs."

She's not better than you.
Maybe just as good.

He laughs, but I already
knew he was kidding.

I wasn't kidding, though.
She might just be better.

To Beat the Heat

The game begins at nine a.m.
We're all glad about that,
because it's pretty warm already.

Coach Tom starts me,
and I pitch well until my arm
starts to get tired.

Cat takes over then, and
she pitches like a champ, too.

It's zero to zero
until the last inning.

Some people call games
like this "pitchers' duels."
Others call them boring
because there isn't a lot
of action on the field.

It's the bottom of the sixth,
and last, inning. The Pirates are up.
Cat throws a hard pitch.
Bram can't keep it
in his catcher's glove.
It bounces to the backstop,
and the batter goes to first
on a passed ball.

Our whole team groans.
You can feel the energy shift.

"Don't give up!" I yell.

Here comes the next batter.
Cat throws a strike.
A ball.
Another strike.

The batter connects
with the fourth pitch,
but he doesn't hit hard.

It should be an easy out,
but the third baseman
bobbles it, then throws
over the head of our second
baseman. The ball rolls
into the outfield.

The Pirates score.
And that's the game.

Not to mention
the playoffs.

Our team finishes
the year in second place.

Not bad.
Just not good enough.

Hopefully

Cat and I will be more
than good enough to ace
the Great Robotics Challenge,
which is the following Saturday.

It won't be easy.
Students from all over Nevada
are traveling to Vegas
to participate.

That's a whole lot of kids.
Not to mention robots.

In a way, maybe it's okay
that we didn't make
the Little League playoffs,
or we would've had to decide
between that and this.

It would've been impossible
to show up for both.

You'd think adults
could figure out stuff better.
I guess not all teachers
are Little League fans.

Doesn't matter.
Not a problem this year.

Dad Drops Me Off

In front of the community
center at 9:45 a.m.

> *I'm so, so sorry I can't stay*
> *and watch. It's just—*

"I know. You have to make up
for those days you took off
for Will, and for our vacation."

> *Exactly. When did you turn*
> *into an adult, anyway?*

"Dad, I'm twelve. Don't rush me."

> *Ha-ha. Okay. Someone will*
> *take videos, though, right?*

"Pretty sure everyone will."

> *Will promised he'd pick you*
> *up and keep his phone on.*
> *Call him as soon as you know*
> *when you'll be finished.*

"I will. And I'll still have to wait.
But it's okay. I'm used to it.
Oh, there's Ms. Pérez, my science
teacher, and our group.
See you on the far side."

I Join My Classmates

And we go inside.
Ms. Pérez and Mr. Banks,
our computer science
teacher, have already
transported our bots
and set up an area
for us to get organized.

Cat and I walk together,
dodging nervous kids
and overwhelmed teachers
and carts of equipment.

*I didn't think there'd be
so many people!* says Cat.

"I did. Remember the YouTube
videos we watched about
those other challenges?"

*Yeah, but it's different
for real, you know?*

Good point. There's so much
to see, your eyes don't know
where to focus. A steady buzz of
talking and hundreds of feet
slapping fills the huge rooms
with noise. And there's
an energy, almost like
electricity, bouncing around.

We get to the designated
RRCS "corral" and Ms. Pérez
goes over the schedule.
Different pairs, with their bots,
will participate in certain challenges
during the day, and when
we're not competing, we need
to root for our teammates.

Cat and I, plus Strike 'Em Out,
will have two different
challenges. The first,
called the Brick Bash,
requires our bot to grab
projectiles, toss them
over a barrier, and knock
over a Lego wall. Head to
head with another robot,
the first to deconstruct
the wall wins the challenge.

> *You take lead on this one,*
> Cat tells me. *I'll be better*
> *at Hit the Bullseye.*

That's our second challenge,
which is pretty much like
throwing baseball strikes,
only with smaller balls.

It's a Great Day

Not only for Strike 'Em Out,
who conquers both challenges,
but also for our entire team.
Out of all the schools here,
we finish in a three-way
tie for first place.

Go, Rainbow Ridge Charter!

It's not like we win money
or anything, but we do get
a nice trophy, or we will
once the event makes two
more. They didn't think
about ties, I guess.

I called Will about an hour
before I expected to be finished.
He didn't pick up, so I left
a message in his voice mail
and as a text. I tried again
thirty minutes later.
Same results.

And now we're finished.
Everything is packed up
and our teachers want
to go home.

Will's not here.
No text. No call.

It's nothing new.
Not a big surprise.
Just, I'm not sure what
I should do.

Try to call Dad?

Cat's still here.
Standing right next to me.
Waiting here with me.

No Will, huh?

"Nope."

*Want a ride? Dad says
we can take you home.*

He and Nicolás are standing
by the front doors, looking
a little impatient.

"Are you sure?"

Yeah. Come on.

I get to ride in Victor
Sánchez's car! How cool
is that? Guess I'll have to
thank Will for forgetting me.

As We Follow

Cat's dad and brother
to the parking lot, I ask,
"Where's your mom?"

       Back in LA.

"For good?"

       No. She's getting the house
       there ready to sell.

"So, she's moving to Vegas?"

       That's the plan, yes.

"I'm glad." I am, for Cat.
"I hope Mateo is okay, too."

       He's not. He'll be in jail
       for a long time, Dad says.

"Maybe he could join the army
instead," I joke, thinking about Mr. C.

       She giggles. I don't think
       the army would want him.

"You never know."

We hop into the back seat
of Victor Sánchez's silver Lexus.

Unlike Becky the 'Vette's
older leather, these seats
are super soft. I sink down
into the cushion for the comfy
ride home. I wish it was longer.

I still can't believe I know
Victor Sánchez, let alone
that I'm friends with his daughter.

It's like sports stars are real
people, too. And, I guess, rock
stars, since one is dating Mom.

"Turn right at the next road,
then take your second left."
I direct him to our house.
Will's car is parked in front.

                    Will you be okay?

"Yeah. Looks like my brother
is here. Thanks for the ride."

                    No problem. You two did well
                    today. I'm proud of you both.
                    I see a lot of talent in you,
                    especially on the baseball field.

My face super-heats.
"Thank you!"

I Kind of Walk on Air

To the door,
though I'd rather
jump up and down.
I can't believe Victor Sánchez
thinks I've got talent.

Wow!
Can't wait to tell Dad and
Grandpa. And maybe brag
a little to Bram.

Hey. I can tell Will
right now.

He probably won't care,
but trying would be
better than stuffing
this crazy-good feeling
inside, where it
just might explode.

"Hey, Will!"
I fling the door open.
"Guess what!"

No answer.
No "Be right there."
Not even "Buzz off!"
No noise at all.
Usually, there's music,
at least.

Maybe he's in the kitchen?
Nope. Empty.
The bathroom?
Nope. Door's wide open.

"Will?" I knock on
his bedroom door.

No answer.

I open it a crack.
Hear nothing.
But when I peek
around it, I can see
Will's Nikes.
On his feet.
On his bed.

He's asleep.
At four thirty in
the afternoon?
Something isn't right.

"Will!"
He doesn't even stir.

I cross the room
in three long steps,
and suddenly the vinegar
taste of fear fills my mouth.

I Shake My Brother

Softly at first, then harder.
He doesn't open his eyes.
I can't wake him.

His skin is gray.
He's barely breathing,
and there's a weird
rattling noise in his chest
when he tries.

I notice a pill bottle
on his nightstand.
Totally empty.

What do I do?
What do I do?

I grab my phone,
call 911. "Help!
I think my brother
took too many pills.
I think he's dying!"

The lady asks me
some questions.
I sputter nonanswers.
She says the ambulance
is on the way.

But what if he needs
help sooner?

What do I do?
What do I do?

Call Dad, for one thing.
I leave an urgent message.

I go to the window
to look for the ambulance,
notice the lights on in
the house next door.

Mr. Cobb!

I run as fast as my legs
can go, ring his bell
over and over.

"Mr. Cobb! Help!"

The door opens right away.

　　　　Trace. What is it?

"Please hurry. Something's
wrong with Will. I called
911 and they're coming."

He doesn't say a word,
just dashes behind me.
I never knew he could
move so quickly.

We Leave the Front Door Open

For the paramedics.
Rush down the hallway
to Will's room.

He still hasn't moved.

"I think it was those."
I point to the pill bottle.

Mr. Cobb ignores that,
puts an ear to Will's chest.
I notice the gurgling noise
in there has stopped.

> *Keep talking to him, Trace.*
> *Tell him to wake up now.*

Mr. Cobb sticks a couple
of fingers into Will's mouth,
and when he pulls them out,
some kind of thick liquid
comes with them.

"Wake up, Will. I want to tell
you about Strike 'Em Out."

Now Mr. Cobb tilts Will's head
backward. Pinches his nose.

"What are you doing?"

> *Rescue breathing.*

That means mouth-to-mouth,
which means Will isn't
breathing on this own.

I start to cry. I can't help it.
But I tell Will about how
our bot threw ten perfect
bull's-eye strikes in a row.

Mr. Cobb keeps filling
Will's lungs with air.

When I hear voices in
the front room, I run
to show them the way.
"In here! In here!"

Two EMTs—one guy,
one girl—take over for
Mr. Cobb, who leads me
out of Will's room.

> Let them work. We don't
> want to get in their way.
> Have you talked to your dad?

"Not yet. He's working.
I left him a message."

> They'll need a parent. Let's call
> the casino. It's an emergency.

I Never Thought of That

I'm glad Mr. Cobb's here.
Some things need adults
to take care of them.

He gets hold of Dad.
The guy paramedic talks
to him on the phone, tells him
what's going on and what
hospital to meet them at.

"Can I go with him?"

> *Probably not the best idea,*
> says Mr. Cobb. *They won't
> know anything right away.
> Those waiting rooms are boring.*

"Yeah. Plus, they stink."

> *Some of them do, that's for sure.*

Will leaves the house
strapped to a gurney,
with a mask to help him
breathe over his face.

He's still unconscious,
but as they wheel him by,
I promise I'll tell him all about
the bot challenge next time
I see him. There will be
a next time. There will.

Outside, the ambulance
turns on its red and blue
lights and disappears down
the block. It's still super warm,
but I have to shake off a chill.

"He's going to be okay, right?"

> I think so, Trace. It's a good
> thing you got here when
> you did, though.

"The good Lord works in
mysterious ways?"

> That he does, son. That he does.
> Hey. You hungry? I was just
> going to make some dinner.

"I haven't eaten since lunch,
but I'm not sure my stomach
is very interested in food."

> Well, how about if I make us
> something, and you can eat
> if you feel like it? Then maybe
> we could watch a movie?

"Okay." It's nice he wants
to keep me company. I don't
want to be alone right now.
"And thanks, Mr. Cobb."

He Stays With Me

Until Dad gets home.
Mr. Cobb is dozing
in the recliner and I'm
fighting sleep, watching
some old comedy show,
when Dad stumbles in.

I'm home.

"Dad!" I bolt upright.
"Is Will okay?"

For now.

For now?
"What does that mean?"

It means he's holding on.

Still unconscious? asks Mr. Cobb.

Yes. It was touch and go.
He coded, but they were
able to resuscitate.

Coded? Like in the movies?
"You mean he almost died?"

Dad nods. *He still could.*

Do they know what happened?

Opioid overdose. Unknown
if it was intentional or accidental.

"Intentional? You mean
maybe he took too many
pills on purpose?"

It's possible.

I have to let it sink in.
Down through layers
of believing everything
was okay, if not exactly
good. Bad, maybe, but . . .

"No way he wanted to die."

That can't be true.
We would've seen it.
I would've known it.

Depressed, yes.
Withdrawn, yes.
Mad at the world.
Reckless.
Fearful.
In pain.

I can understand those things.
I can't understand wanting to die.

He Could Still Die

If he did, I wouldn't
even get a chance
to say goodbye.

When was the last time
he and I talked?

What did I say to him?
Was it mean?

Did I tease him?
Insult him?
Make him feel bad?

I can't remember.
Think, Trace, think.

I didn't see him
at breakfast, so it must
have been last night.

For dinner we had . . .
toaster waffles, with peanut
butter and honey.
When he sat at the table,
change jingled in his pocket.

That reminded me
that he still owes the money
he took, but did I say anything
about that? No, it was . . .

Right Before We Ate

I had just finished
playing my keyboard.

I guess music is kind
of like pills for me.

It takes me to a place
where I can lose
my anger
by playing hard,
or find logic
in its math and order
when everything
seems a little crazy.

It brings me peace.
And that's what
I was thinking.

Will came through
the living room on
his way to the kitchen.

"Hey, Will. Why don't you
ever play guitar anymore?"

Mom taught him how
when he was little, and
he used to play all the time.
I remember him strumming
some of her music.

Sometimes they played
and sang together.

I gave up on guitar
when Mom gave up on me.

"That's dumb."

Not really. It reminds
me of before. When life
kept a steady rhythm.

"You should start again.
It might make you happy."

What's the point of being
happy? I can't even smile.

He hardly ever talks about
that. I guess I'm just so used
to the way his face works
(or doesn't) that I forget
he lost that part of himself.

For most people,
a lost smile is temporary,
something easily fixed
with a joke, a funny video,
or even just a kind word.
It's hard to imagine
losing one forever.

I should've been nicer,
should have offered
a kind word or ten.

But what I said was
"Stop feeling sorry for yourself.
You can always smile inside."

His eye roll was huge,
and when he answered,
he was snotty.

> *Interior smiling. Gotcha.*
> *I'll get right to work on that.*

Pretty Sure

That was the last thing
I said to him, although
when he yelled to come
get a waffle for dinner
I might have told him
to make me two.

I should've
                said I was sorry.

Should've
                thanked him for
                toasting the waffles.

Should've
                asked him to play
                a video game.

Should've
                mentioned how much
                I'd like him to come
                watch the bot challenge.

Should've
                told him I don't care
                if he can't smile or that
                his right cheek twitches,
                don't care if he forgets
                me sometimes.

Because I love him.

Mr. Cobb Clears His Throat

Yanks me out of yesterday,
back into this terrible moment.

*I'll leave the two of you
alone,* he says. *Unless
you need me for something.*

Not right now, answers Dad.
*But thanks for everything.
I don't know how to repay you.*

*Don't worry about that.
Glad for what I could do.*

"Hey, Mr. Cobb? The grilled
cheese was really good."

He winks. *Wait till you taste
my scrambled eggs.*

Before he goes, he lays
a hand on my shoulder.

*Positive thoughts. Your
brother will be okay.*

The door closes behind him.

Touch and go.
Holding on.
For now.

Where do I hunt
for positive thoughts?

Sifting through desert sand?
The Sahara?
Death Valley?
Just east of Vegas?

Beneath mountain snow?
Mount Olympus?
Mammoth?
Tahoe?

Mom.
She should know.

I ask Dad if he tried
to get hold of her.

> *Yes. Left her a message.*
> *I'll try again, but it's late.*
> *Get some sleep if you can.*
> *Tomorrow will be a long day.*

I take the time to give
Dad a big hug.

At least I can tell him,
"I love you."

Somehow

I must have fallen asleep
because I wake to the smell
of fresh brewed coffee.

When I follow my nose,
I find Mr. Cobb in the kitchen,
holding a big mug of the stuff.

> *Your dad went to the hospital*
> *early and asked if I'd stay*
> *with you until he gets back.*

"Does this mean I get to
try your scrambled eggs?"

> *If you're hungry, you bet.*
> *While I work on them, I left*
> *something for you there on the table.*

It's a small box.
Inside is a medallion
on a yellow ribbon with
red and green stripes.

"What is it?"

> *My Vietnam Service Medal.*

I study it carefully. There's
a dragon kind of hiding
behind some bamboo.

And sure enough, it says:
REPUBLIC OF VIETNAM SERVICE

"But . . . why give it to me?"

> *I've got no one to leave it to.*
> *Leona and I never had kids.*
> *Too busy working our lives away.*

> *Maybe it will give you courage.*
> *Maybe it will bring you good luck.*
> *Seems like you could use some*
> *of both right about now.*

My eyes sting suddenly.
I don't know what to say.
I mumble, "Thank you,"
but that's not enough.

Without even thinking,
I jump up, run over, and
give him a huge hug.
"I'll take good care of it."

> *I have no doubt about that.*
> *Now, let's have breakfast.*

His scrambled eggs
are awesome.

Will Hangs On

But he isn't "out of
the woods," as Grandpa
calls it, for a few days.

Meanwhile, our house
fills with people.
Plus one dog.

Lily.
Grandpa.
Clara.

They all hang out,
taking turns,
so I'm never alone.

Dad's at the hospital a lot.
But he tries to work, too.

> *I need to keep my job.*
> *Plus, it takes my mind*
> *off things I can't change.*

I go to school,
but it's hard to focus.
Luckily, we're closing
in on the end of the year,
so it's mostly review stuff.
Cat and Bram stay close
to me. It's good to have
good friends.

Lily Picks Me Up

From school Tuesday
afternoon. It's been
three days since Will
took too many pills.

He's alive, but still
hooked up to machines,
and I don't get to see him.

When I get in Lily's car,
I don't notice Sylvester
in the back seat until his
cold nose nudges my neck.
I reach back to pet him.

> *He really adores you,* Lily
> says. *I mean, he likes most
> people, but you're definitely
> one of his favorites. I think
> it was doggy love at first sight.*

That makes me smile.
Not many things have
for the past few days.

"Love you, too, Sylvester."
It's supposed to be a joke, but it
might be true. Strong like, anyway.

As we head toward home,
I say, "We've never had pets.

Will wanted a puppy once,
but Mom said she was allergic."

> Some people are. I'm glad
> I'm not. I've always had dogs.
> They're the best because
> they give love unconditionally.

"Good thing Dad's not
allergic, then, I guess."

> Yes, that would make things
> more difficult. I'm not sure
> I could give up either of them.

"You love Dad."

> Very much.

"Why?"

> Because he's kind. Because
> we have fun together.
> And because of how much
> he loves you and your brother.

Good reasons.

> Hey, Trace? I can never replace
> your mom. But I want you to
> know I'm here for you, okay?

Cool

That's what I say.
And that's how I try
to act, even though
I'd kind of like to cry.

I need someone
here for me.

Someone besides Dad,
who can't always be.

Someone besides Mom,
who divorced herself
from Will and me,
as well as from Dad.

Someone besides Will,
who has forgotten
the bond of family.

I feel like a kite
come loose from its string
and its tail tangled up
in a very tall tree.

No way to rescue it
unless a perfect
whisp of wind
plucks it just right,
sets it free.

It's Wednesday

By the time Mom finally
gets here. Four days.
Apparently she and Rory
Davis were on some "silent
retreat" near Tahoe.

No phones. No electronics.
Just the two of them
communing with nature,
which I guess means
talking to the squirrels
and birds and stuff.

I'm in my last class
of the day when the school
secretary calls me down
to be picked up by a parent.
My first thought is it's Dad,
and if he's picking me up,
something terrible happened.

But when I get to the office,
it's a beautiful woman with
silver-tipped hair standing there.
And no matter that it's been
five months since I've seen her,
or that she never let me
know she was on her way,
I run the last few steps to reach her.

"Mama."

No Clue

Where that came from.
If I ever called her "Mama"
before, it was a long, long
time ago. I don't care.

She opens her arms,
and I tumble into them,
inhaling a familiar scent
of rosemary and vanilla.
She still uses the same shampoo!

>*I just came from the hospital.*
>*Your brother turned the corner*
>*this morning. He'll be okay.*

I stiffen.
I mean, I'm glad Will's better.
Of course I am. I've dreaded
bad news for days now.

But couldn't she give a few
minutes just to me?

"Yay! I bet it's because of you."

>*I don't think so. It happened*
>*before I got there.*
>*But everyone is very relieved.*
>*You ready? Rory's out front.*

"You brought Rory Davis?"

Well, actually, he brought me.
We drove down as soon as we heard.

I don't know how to feel.

Happy
  because she's here.
Mad
  because she's not alone.
Relieved
  because Will's okay.
Irritated
  because he's the only reason
  she came at all.

She takes my hand
to lead me outside.

Her skin is cool and soft
and it calls a memory.

I'm a little kid,
holding on tight
to my mom so
    I
    don't
    get
    lost.

This Range Rover

Is extra, extra big.
I have to really climb
to make it up inside.

Aren't these things supposed
to go everywhere? Because, for a huge
four-wheel-drive, it's pretty fancy.

The tall man in the driver's seat
turns, pushing a strand of super-
long gray hair off his ski-tanned face.

> *You must be Trace,* he says. *Your*
> *mom's told me so much about you.*

Somehow I doubt that, but
at least he's got the right name.

"And you're Rory Davis.
She didn't mention you, but
everyone knows who you are."

> *I started to tell you last time*
> *we talked, but you interrupted me.*

Sure. My fault. How Mom.
Am I supposed to apologize?
I'll change the subject instead.

"When can I see Will?"

Not for a while, says Mom.
He's still kind of out of it.

"How long are you staying?"

A couple of days. We'll be
looking into some rehab
programs for your brother.

"Rehab? You mean,
like, drug counseling?"

I've been talking to your dad.
We agree an inpatient situation
would probably be best for him.

At least they're talking,
I guess, but I don't much like
what they're discussing.

"You mean like a hospital."

Something like that, though
he wouldn't be confined to a bed.

"But he couldn't leave."

Will is sick, Trace. He needs
serious help he can't get at home.

I Always Believed

Pills were to make you
better. I never thought
they could be a sickness.

One question nags at me.
"Was it intentional, Mom?"

> *We still don't know. He's not*
> *talking about it yet.*

> *That might take a while,*
> *says Rory Davis. And he*
> *might not even be sure.*

"How could he not be sure?"

> *Sometimes you forget*
> *how much you've ingested.*

"How do you know?"

> *Because I've been there.*
> *I've been sober for six years.*
> *Recovery is possible, but it requires*
> *a strong desire to succeed.*

"I hope he wants to."

> *We all do, Trace. He'll need*
> *our support for sure. We all*
> *have to be there for him.*

But That Doesn't Mean

Mom plans to stick around.
She stays long enough
to find a rehab place for Will.
It's in California, close to the beach.

Rory (I get to call him that
now) says the atmosphere
is important. And Mom agrees.

It's a beautiful place.

"How long will he be there?"

It's a six-month program.

"Six months? What about school?"

*Summer vacation starts
in a couple of weeks. After
that, he'll have classes there.*

"But why so long?"

*Opioid dependency is tough
to beat,* explains Rory.
*He'll need a lot of professional
help to understand why he started
using in the first place.*

*Plus, he'll be far away from
the people he's been buying from.*

People Like the Vampire

The idea is, by the time
Will comes home,
those dealers, as Mom
calls them, will have
moved on. Hopefully
all the way to jail.

Rory and Mom are going
to drive Will to the rehab
center. They pick him up
from the hospital on Saturday
and stop by the house so
he can pack some stuff
and say goodbye.

Everyone wanted to be
here, but Will insisted
it just be Dad and me.
When he comes in,
he's pale as paper,
and his hands tremble.

Rory said he might be shaky.
His body is fighting him,
demanding the pills
he can't have anymore.

I want to cry. But I'll act
cool. "Hey, Will."

Uh . . . Hi.

"You doing okay?"

                    Been better. But I'll survive.

That is the point. "Good.
Where's Mom and Rory?"

                    They went to gas up the SUV.
                    I've only got a half hour,
                    so I'd better start packing.

"Lily already washed
and folded your clothes.
They're on your bed."

I don't mention how she
and Dad went through
everything in his room
to make sure he didn't
have any pills stashed.

                    Where's Dad?

Just as he asks, the lawn mower
snarls and a green perfume
floats through the window.

"Out back. Want me to get him?"

                    When I'm finished.

I Trail Will to His Room

Not that he asked me to.

Spying on me?

I could say something
mean, or make a joke.
But I'm honest when I
tell him, "I only get to see
you for a little while."

You saying you'll miss me?

I turn my head
so he can't see the hot drip
of tears, and I cough, "Uh-huh."

He opens the suitcase
that's sitting beside the bed,
starts filling it with socks.

"Don't forget your Jockeys."

Underwear. Check.

"Hey, Will? I'm sorry."

For what?

I've had time to think
about this. "For not noticing
sooner. And for not saying

something right away
when I finally did."

Why didn't you?

"I wanted to protect you."

*That's not your job, little
brother. Refuse the guilt!*

A hint of a sense of humor.
Shades of the old Will.

"But . . . what could I have
done? To stop you, I mean."

He quits feeding clothes
into his suitcase. Flips his dark
hair, which has grown too long,
off his forehead, out of his eyes.

*Listen, Trace. You can't stop
anyone who's determined
to go down a certain path.*

*You can tell them you think
it's wrong. That you're scared
for them, even. But you can't
stop them because decisions
like that are totally their own.*

*The best you can do
is keep loving them.*

That Will Take Time

To process completely.
Time I don't have right now.

What I know for sure
is "I love you, Will."

I know. You, too. I always
have. I'm sorry if I ever
made you feel otherwise.

The pills made me forget
about the pain, but also about
the things that were important
to me. Especially the people.

"Hey, Will. Are you scared?"

Yeah.

That makes me scared for him.
Funny, I don't get scared
very often. Once, though . . .

"Remember that time
we were snowboarding
and took a wrong turn?
We ended up at the top
of a really steep run.
I was afraid to go down it.
Remember what you said?"

He thinks a minute. Nods.

> *I said sometimes you have to*
> *have faith in yourself, step over*
> *the edge, and take the plunge.*

"I did. Actually, I put my faith
in you. I took the plunge. I fell.
But I picked myself up and made it
to the bottom. Then we went
back up and took the run again."

> *And you fell again.*

"But I didn't the next time.
I figured out my mistakes
and corrected them."

> *Yeah, well, you're pretty*
> *smart. For a dumb kid.*

"So, you took a wrong
turn. You can fix it."

But now I see.
I can't.

Will Goes to His Closet

Digs around, returns
with a favorite pair
of Adidas, and swaps
them for the fancy Nikes
he has on his feet.

"What are you doing?"

>He shrugs. *The Adidas are*
>*more comfortable. Anyway,*
>*I was wearing the Nikes when . . .*

They rode in the ambulance
with him. "Right. Hey, Will?
I'm glad you didn't die."

>*Me, too. I think. We'll see.*

That doesn't make me feel
better. But it does make
me glad he's getting help.

My eyes travel across
the room, to the black
case standing in one corner.

"Will they let you bring
your guitar, do you think?"

>*I don't know.*

"You should see."

Maybe you should pawn it
for the money I owe you.

Guessing he could tell
me where the nearest
pawnshop happens to be.

Also guess I need to forgive
him. Like, all the way.

"I'll make you a deal.
Take your guitar and you
don't have to pay me back."

I don't get it. Why?

"Because music is medicine.
And also because if Mom
never gives you anything
else, she gave you that.
And it's special."

He's not convinced.
Time will tell, I suppose.

But when he puts his suitcase
next to the front door,
he puts his guitar case beside it.

Dad Comes In

Decorated with sprays
of fresh-cut grass.

> *Getting hot out there,*
> *he says. You're lucky*
> *you'll be near the water*
> *for the summer.*

> *Not sure how much time*
> *I'll get to spend at the beach.*

> *Well, at least you'll have*
> *the ocean breeze.*

I think this is what's known
as small talk. It's what you do
when you're scared you might
say something wrong, so instead
you discuss the weather.

Outside the window, I see
the Range Rover pull up against
the curb. "Mom's here."

Dad walks Will to the door.
Gives him a giant bear hug.

> *You can do this, son. Don't*
> *hesitate to let me know*
> *if you need anything at all.*

Sure, Dad.

"Hey! You should have Rory
Davis autograph your guitar."
Brilliant idea. "Just don't pawn it."

Dad looks kind of horrified,
but a small laugh escapes Will.

*No pawnshops where
I'm going, Trace.*

The bell rings.
I open the door.
Mom steps inside.

For one small moment,
the four of us are together.

For one small moment,
it's like she never left.

One tiny moment.

Dad tells Will he loves him.
Will tells Dad he loves him.
Mom tells me she loves me.

"Love you, Mom.
You too, Will."

Dad and I

Stand at the open door,
watching them go
until the Range Rover
turns the corner and
disappears from sight.

"Will's going to get better
now, right, Dad?"

> It's totally up to him at this point.
> Listen, Trace. If you ever again
> think something's wrong, you keep
> telling me until you're sure
> I understand what you're saying.

"Okay."

> Promise?

"Promise."

I make a promise
to myself, too.

I will never cover for Will
again, or for anyone else.
At least not over
something this big.

Some secrets
shouldn't be kept.

As We Close the Door

And retreat inside, my phone
buzzes in my pocket.

The message is from Cat:

> *How's Will?*

I text back:

On his way to rehab.
Looks pretty good.
Says he's scared.

> *How are you?*

Worried for him.
Glad he's alive.

> *Anytime you want*
> *to talk, I'm here.*

Thanks, Cat.

I kind of want to hang
out with her now.
Maybe go to the batting
cages or something.

Having friends is one thing.
Having friends who stick
by you, no matter what,
                    is everything.

It's Sunday Afternoon

Eight days
since Will
almost died.

He's gone.
But he'll be back.
Still, his room is empty.

And so is a space inside me.
There's a hole, a hollow,
and it won't be filled
until he returns,
wanting to stay alive.

I've got friends.
Family.
A decent next-door neighbor.
Even a part-time dog.
All of them are good to me.
But Will is my brother.

I'm on the couch, studying
for finals. Dad sits next to me.

> *There's a game on soon,* he says.
> *And later Lily's coming to dinner.*
> *I want to talk to you about*
> *something before she gets here.*

"Good or bad?"

Good, at least I think so.

I put my book on the coffee
table, look at Dad, who's all
serious. "What is it?"

*I've been thinking about buying
a diamond ring for Lily.
But only with your permission.*

I swallow hard. "You want
to get married. And you
want me to say it's okay."

*I think you know how I feel about her.
She and I have been talking.
We want to become a real family.
But only if you want that, too.*

Just a month ago I would've
said no. In fact, I probably
would've yelled it. I could use
a little time to process, though.

"Can I think about it?"

*Dad smiles. Of course. Take
as long as you need. I mean,
not like years or anything.*

I Take My Schoolbooks

Back to my bedroom,
put them on my desk.
Sit in the chair by my window.

I see Mr. Cobb opening
his garage door, think of
his Corvette beneath
her custom cover, and
his words float into my mind.

Becky is the love of my life.
Well, there was one other . . .

Becky is still there for him,
but she's just a car, even if
she is super-duper special.

The "one other" is gone now,
and he can't ever have her back.
Some things you can't fix,
no matter how much you want to.
He must get awful lonely.

I wouldn't want that
for Grandpa.
I'm glad he has Clara.
I wouldn't want that
for Dad.
I'm glad he has Lily.

I'm Glad

Because I've spent
a lot of time alone
here in this house,
but I knew eventually
someone would come
                    home.

But I won't always
live with Dad.
Will won't, either.
We might move
far away from
                    home.

Maybe to the mountains.
To ski or snowboard.

            Maybe to the ocean.
            To play music at the beach.

                        Maybe to Minnesota.
                        To grow food on a farm.

Who knows?
But while we're
figuring out where
we want to go,
I wouldn't want Dad
to be alone.

Mom Isn't Coming Back

She could barely step
through the door
and hang out for
a couple of minutes.

I wish things could be
different, but wishes
don't always come true.

Maybe I'll see her this summer.
But even if I do, it won't be
her and Will and me, hiking
or mountain biking.

It won't even just be her
and me. It will always
be her and her music.
And maybe her and Rory.
That's something else I can't fix.

I go to my closet.
Way in back, behind
the stack of Lego boxes,
is the bottle of shampoo
and the magazines.

I leave the shampoo.
Someday I might
want that reminder
of my mother's
hair perfume.

As for the magazines,
I turn to the articles
featuring Mom that
I've looked at dozens
of times. I know them
word for word, by heart.

And that's where
I decide to leave them.
In my heart.
I can't quite bring
myself to throw
them away, though.

Dad yells, *Hey, Trace! Game's
about to start. LA at Colorado.
Should be a good one.*

Colorado. That gives me
an idea. I take the magazines
to the living room, where
the game is just underway.

"Hey, Dad? Can we mail
these to Maureen and Paul?
They might want them
for a scrapbook or something."

When he sees what they are,
he asks if I'm sure, and I nod.
"Positive."

Bottom of the Ninth

The Dodgers are creaming the Astros,
10–2, when Lily and Sylvester
come through the door. With pizza.

Dad gets up to give Lily a kiss,
but before he does, he looks
in her eyes and says softly,

I love you.

She glances my way,
and I realize she's wondering
if it's okay with me. Yes or no,
she kisses him back, whispers,

Love you, too.

So, yeah, they love each other,
and I see now that it doesn't mean
less love for me. It means more.
And there's no such thing as too
much love, only too little.

Sylvester trots over for a pet,
and when he nuzzles my hand,
kind of pushing it up toward
the top of his head, I understand
this dog is asking for love.

I've got plenty to give him,
and I think he's got lots for me.

As the last Astro batter folds
and the Dodgers win, Lily takes
the pizza into the kitchen.
Sylvester follows, probably
hoping for a stray piece
of pepperoni or cheese.

That hollow place
Mom and Will left
behind shrinks a little.

This isn't the family
I grew up with, the one
I tried to stitch back together
when it came unraveled.
But this one isn't bad.

Dad starts toward the kitchen.
"Wait," I tell him. "About you
and Lily. I guess it's okay.
But you have to wait at least
six months, so you're sure."

Dad grins. *Okay, Trace.*
We all want to be sure.
Six months seems reasonable.
Now, let's get some pizza.

Dad Knows

Being sure is not
the real reason
I want them to wait.

They definitely are,
and I am mostly
sure along with them.

But this is huge.
Not just for me,
but for all of us
who are part of
this expanding family.

We are growing,
despite losing one.
Mom will always be
important to me, but
we can move on without her.

If Dad and Lily's wedding
is in our future, all the rest
of us have to be there.
That will take six months.
We can't move forward
without my brother.

And so,
one more time . . .
                    What about Will?

Author's Note

FAMILY DYNAMICS ARE personal, and always thought-provoking. My husband and I are currently raising a third generation of kids. Gen One: way-adult children, two daughters and a son. Growing up, the girls related to each other, but not so much to their older brother.

Gen Two: adopted only-child son, who did all the things—school, sports, music (metal?!), lots of travel—and built deep friendships but lacked sibling connections.

Gen Three: our grandchildren. And with them, for the first time, we are watching the relationship between brothers, almost five years apart.

This book is a tribute to the younger of the two, who has grown up in the very long shadow of his troubled brother. To love someone and watch them struggle is hard. It's even more difficult when your own accomplishments too often go unrecognized because the spotlight is shining on someone else's problems. And yet you soldier on, earning straight A's, pitching Little League no-hit innings, and singing your way through every day, because that is who you are.

With or without siblings, whatever their circumstances, every child deserves recognition. If raising one "takes a village," we'd better build galaxies.

Turn the page for more
from Ellen Hopkins

Definition of *Resent*:
Feel Bothered By

Cal moved in
a little more than a year ago.
He wasn't exactly a stranger.

Aunt Caryn was his mom,
and she and my mom were more
than sisters. They were identical twins.

> *Two halves of a whole,*
> Mom called them.

They were close, but they
didn't live near each other.
Aunt Caryn moved to Arizona
before Cal was born.

She visited once in a while
and came to a couple of family
reunions. Talk about trouble!

I guess when Aunt Caryn met
Cal's dad and dropped out
of college, it made Grandma mad.

> *They hardly talk at all anymore,*
> Mom told me once. *And when*
> *they do, they end up shouting.*

"So why does Aunt Caryn
go to the reunions?" I asked.
"Grandma's always there."

> Caryn still wants to be part
> of the family, and she wants
> Cal to know his relatives.

"I think Grandma should
forgive her," I said.

> I think so, too. But my mother
> has a hard time with forgiveness.
> She thinks it's a sign of weakness.

Grandma still hadn't forgiven
her when Aunt Caryn died.

I'll never forget that day.
Mom cried and cried.
When she finally stopped,
her face was so puffed up,
I could barely see her eyes.

> I lost a piece of myself, she said.

Maybe Cal living with us
is like getting that piece back.

Maybe that's why Mom lets him
get away with everything,
from pranks to meltdowns to lies.
I'm sorry, but I resent that.

> *Try to find a little sympathy,*
> Mom urges. *After Caryn passed,*
> *things got pretty rough for Cal.*

His dad took him after
the funeral, but the details
of the next two years are a mystery.
And no one's giving out clues.

> *You'll have to wait for Cal to tell*
> *you,* Mom says. *It's not up to me.*

Whatever happened, I feel sorry
for Cal. If my mom died, I'd be lost.
Cal must feel lost sometimes, too.
So, yeah, I want to forgive his quirks.

Definition of *Quirk*:
Weird Habit

Still, Cal isn't easy to live
with. I like order. Routine.
He's the king of chaos.

Our spare room is Cal's lair
now. Mom let him paint it
charcoal and doesn't even
yell about the mess—
greasy wrappers here,
dirty clothes there.
Imagine what's crawling
around in his closet!
                            Gross.

I have to share a bathroom
with him, which might not
be so bad, except he forgets
to drop the toilet seat.
I've splashed down
in the dark
more than once.
                            Gross squared.

Cal drinks milk straight
from the carton,
and brushes his teeth
without toothpaste.
Sometimes he doesn't
brush them at all.
                            Gross cubed.

Those are little things.

But Cal has bigger problems.
Like right now at school,
we're outside for recess.

It never gets really cold here,
but it's early November. The sky
is gray and the air is kind of sharp.
Almost everyone is playing ball.

> Softball.
> > Kickball.
> > > Tetherball.
> > > > Basketball.

But Cal is sitting against
a wall of the sixth-grade
building, face in a book.
He reads, like, three a week.

Our teacher, Mrs. Peabody,
keeps telling him to slow down.

> *Comprehension means more
> than word count,* she says.

But, no. He *has* to read more
than anyone else, and asks
for books that are *long* and
advanced. Sometimes it seems
like he's showing off.

The problem with that
is it can draw the attention
of bullies, especially those
who think it's hilarious
to make someone freak out.

There go two now,
and they're headed
in Cal's direction.

This could be bad.

Definition of *Intervene*:
Get Involved

Vic Malloy is
    taller than average
    square
    buzz-cut
    meaner than snot.

Bradley Jones is
    a head shorter
    round
    faux-hawked
    meaner than snot.

They close in on Cal.
I know what they've got in mind.
Cal's been in this school
for a year. They've seen
him melt down before.

I nudge my best friend
Misty, who's watching
the tetherball wind
and unwind around the pole.

"Look."

Uh-oh, she says.

We're all the way across
the field, so we can't hear
what the boys are saying.
But when Cal looks up,
his expression is easy to read.

Annoyed.
Anxious.
Angry.

Think we should intervene?
Misty asks. *Like the counselor
told us to do in that assembly?*

"Yeah. We probably should."

But before we can, Vic kicks
the book, and when it goes
flying, Cal jumps to his feet.
The other boys laugh
and move in toward him.

Some kids might respond
by raising their fists.
Others might shrink back
against the wall.

Cal screams.
Like a siren.

                                    Piercing.
                          Panicky.
                Painful.

Everyone stops
what they're doing.
Turns to stare.

The playground-duty
teachers go running.

Vic and Bradley
slink off into the shadows.
Laughing hysterically.

                    And Cal
                    is still screaming.

Definition of *Mortified*:
Totally Embarrassed

Our principal, Mr. Love
(yeah, I know), comes
to see what the problem is.

He puts an arm around
Cal's shoulders, steers
him toward the office.

> *Well, that was special,*
> says Misty. *Your cousin*
> *is weird, you know.*

My cheeks were already
hot. Now they're on fire.
"Hey, it's not *my* fault."

> Misty sniffs. *I didn't say*
> *it was your fault.*
> *No one thinks that.*

"So why is everyone looking
at me? I'm mortified!"

> *Hannah, you're the most*
> *popular girl in the sixth grade.*
> *Don't even worry about it.*

"Okay, fine." But my face
is still burning when the bell
rings and we go back inside.

Luckily, Cal isn't here.
Mr. Love has him working
in the office, where it's quiet.

That's an "accommodation"
of Cal's IEP. That means
Individualized Education Program.

Kids who have a hard time
learning get accommodations. It doesn't
mean they're not smart.

Cal is, for sure. But when
he has a meltdown like that one,
he can't pay attention in class.

Neither can anyone else.
Especially not me. Mom
swears Cal can't control it.

> *His therapist says when*
> *too much comes at him*
> *at once, his brain crashes.*

Crashing brain!
                Siren screaming!
                                Sometimes he throws things.

I get that it's not all his fault.
No one wants to be pushed
aside and made fun of.

I wish I knew how to help
him. I wish I could figure
out how to be his friend.

But that's hard
because I'm not exactly
sure who he really is.

Acknowledgments

WRITING A BOOK is always a semi-lonely pursuit. You spend a lot of time in your own head, not to mention your office or wherever you go to create. So, you might think writing a book during a pandemic-induced stay-at-home lockdown wouldn't be such a big deal. But you'd be wrong.

Almost every writer I know struggled to create during the time I wrote this book, and that includes me. Where words used to flow by the thousands, they sputtered by the dozens. There were days I called myself an imposter and meant it. Had this story not been so important to me, it might never have found its way into these pages. It took the moral support of a number of people, whom I'd like to acknowledge here.

To my family, who listened to me yell, moan, cry, cuss, and whisper to my computer, thank you for your patience, grocery store runs, help in the kitchen, and endless inspiration. To my mutual admiration club—Susan, Susan, Andrew, Amy, Amy, Matt, Laura, and Jim—thank you for those late-night calls and regular Zooms that reminded me I'm a writer second. First, I'm a (good) person, and subject to human frailties. To forever friends and old classmates, thanks for your longtime presence in my life. It's been quite the journey. To my SCBWI clan, you remain a beacon. To readers, teachers, librarians, and all those who support my efforts daily, I appreciate every one of you.

To my agent, Laura Rennert, who always insists I can when I complain I can't, I wouldn't be here without you. And, of course, to my team at Penguin, especially Stacey Barney, this beautiful book is in the world because of you. Thank you for not only being in my corner but for *being* my corner of the publishing world.